THE
ARROWING
OF THE
CANE

JOHN CONYNGHAM

A Fireside Book
Published by Simon & Schuster Inc.
New York London Toronto Sydney Tokyo

FIRESIDE
Simon & Schuster Building
Rockefeller Center
1230 Avenue of the Americas
New York, New York 10020

Copyright © 1986 by John Conyngham

First Fireside Edition, 1989

Published by arrangement with the author.

First published in South Africa by Ad Donker (Pty) Ltd.

FIRESIDE and colophon are registered trademarks
of Simon & Schuster Inc.

Manufactured in the United States of America

10 9 8 7 6 5 4 3 2 1   Pbk.

Library of Congress Cataloging in Publication Data

Conyngham, John.
    The arrowing of the cane / John Conyngham.— 1st Fireside ed.
      p.   cm.
    "A Fireside book."
    I. Title.
PR9369.3.C59A89   1989
823—dc20   89-34424

ISBN 0-671-68755-7   Pbk.

Mysterious fires on South African sugar plantations, plus the discovery of a Boer War diary kept by an ancestor, force cane grower James Colville to realize that both himself and his country are sliding towards a vortex where past and present clash, and life meets death. As liberal Colville struggles to chronicle truthfully his final weeks, his growing spirituality and gradual acceptance of the shortcomings of history, his nation and himself, allow him ultimately to face the end with an impressive equanimity.

The Arrowing of the Cane focuses on the accountability caused by the passage of time; it's steeped with mood and superbly evocative imagery. The conundrum of a white person who can appreciate the black point of view becomes a poignant reminder of the complexities of right and wrong, good and bad.

FOR MIA WOOLLAM, IN MEMORY

Here, traveller, scholar, poet, take your stand
When all those rooms and passages are gone,
When nettles wave upon a shapeless mound
And saplings root among the broken stone.

W.B. Yeats, Cooke Park, 1929

I

It is, I suppose, the beginning of the end. Hundreds of monkeys are trapezing up the valley. With the leopards gone, they have run amuck. Troops scour the trees for fledgelings and eggs. Sorties raid the orchard and steal stalks from the fields of cane adjoining the belts of sub-tropical bush. Plunder, then back to the foliage. Therefore the pressing need to cull. And with all the predators decimated, it has become my task. Ape versus ape. Despite being hopelessly outnumbered, there is fight in me yet. I take my toll.

Burst: the nudge of the recoil and the shattering effect. A vervet claws and stiffens before slipping and falling, crashing through the matting of branches and groundcover. Burst: the sound echoes up and out of the wooded gully and towards the long bungalow on the opposite hillside. The second vervet, caught in mid flight, continues on a lengthened arc, then thuds into the maidenhair. The jabbering has stopped. The bush is deceptively quiet. Two black-collared barbets begin their jaunty duet as the bandarlog conduct a tactical retreat. Deep in the undergrowth they are loping back to a rallying point. Unlike the leopard, I don't have a mate to harry their flanks. The majority must always escape. The best I can hope for is a drop in their morale. Today is mine but the wiliest among them know that tomorrow is another day.

'Sa Brutus!' *The* boxer — he is too much his own to be called *my* — plunges into the bug-weed from the dirt road which runs along the contour on the opposite side of the valley from the bungalow. I release the spent cartridges and lean back against the Land Rover. A whiff of cordite; memories of burning guys and exploded squibs. I light a cheroot and fill my lungs with its muck. Brutus appears with a limp grey form hanging from his jaws. I toss the monkey onto the back of the Land Rover and he returns to the bush.

9

I look out across the valley. Her voice. It calls me from the cane and inwardly I reply, sensing her among the stalks. She wants confirmation of our meeting and I answer in the affirmative: yes Sarah, tonight as usual. How articulate she is. Acute.

I can see our rendezvous in my mind's eye. It is, as always on these occasions, at night. In the distance the swollen tide groans with its burden. After several J&Bs I play my flute on the veranda. The harbinger descends and dances to my music. Slowly Sarah emerges from the cane, moving up through the mangoes and pawpaws to the lawn, keeping just within the fringe of the darkness. We talk, or rather she relates while I listen. Spellbound, I enter her world: Ceylon in the heady days of Empire. The younger daughter of a tea planter of Knuckles Ridge Estate, Matale District, she succumbs at eighteen to my great-great uncle, Lieutenant Harold Colville, 2nd Warwickshire Regiment, in a glossy arbour beyond the coolie lines. Their euphoric honeymoon ends prematurely when a tribe in distant Zululand rejects subjugation and he is called away on active service. Stranded in the hills, she busies herself reading, pressing flowers and collecting butterflies which the gardener catches in traps baited with urine. Occasionally the turbaned postman delivers a letter — a scribbled note about the ponderous advance of Colonel Pearson's column up the Natal coast; the pontoon on the Tugela and the construction of Fort Tenedos on the northern bank; the elusiveness of the enemy and his — Harry's — return to his regiment, part of Lord Chelmsford's central column on its advance to Isandlwana.

All this Sarah tells me until the sight of the nightwatchman's torch bobbing up from the stables sends her sweeping back into the cane, leaving me peering through the saffron lens of my tumbler, seeing everything as if in an old photograph. Perhaps one that Harry took but was later lost.

A distant activity is faintly audible: the singing of working men, the roar of tractors and the rhythmical slash-fall of pangas and cane. A murmuring. Beyond the valley and the rolling foothills smudged with burnt patches lies the sea, a solid blue band yet so fluid and moving.

A crashing in the undergrowth. Brutus returns, dragging a bull monkey whose blue testicles remind me of Christmas tree baubles. I lift both animals onto the Land Rover, wipe blood from my hand onto the thigh of my khaki trousers, and drive to the cutting. The road is sprinkled with gobbets of chewed cane — monkey vandalism. In a gluttonous frenzy, they destroy the cane rows adjacent to the road, tossing complete stalks onto the pinkish gravel. Like man, they are wasteful, never taking only what they need. Therefore the pressing need to cull.

I brake and pull the Land Rover up on the side of the road. Humming some inane rhyme, I climb out and walk across the trash to where the blacks are cutting the cane. An Indian tractor driver backs his trailer up to a stack of cut stalks. Several cutters look up from their work and then continue, slashing the bases of the cane stalks with their pangas. The trailer's winch rattles and the stack shudders, sliding on its steel runners, settling finally on the trailer. A black induna, dressed in a navy blue overall and not in the hessian shift of a cutter, walks towards me as I near the labourers. We exchange greetings and he gives me the stack total and attendance record. His cheeks are lined with tribal scars and his smile reveals a flash of perfect teeth. Charcoal has its merits, minus fluoride and all.

Two cutters are absent. Although they are all extremely fit men, the majority rest for one or two working days a month. Consequently they lose on their monthly bonuses but their basic wages remain unchanged. Each is entitled to several days off if he works well for the remainder of the month. If, however, he needs too much rest without good reason, he becomes a liability and is told to seek another farm where his behaviour is acceptable. I use this method whenever a man's actions warrant his dismissal. I tell him that our ideas differ and that it will be better for everyone if he seeks employment with a planter whose ideas are similar to his. In this way I avoid firing all but the worst offenders. The majority are merely asked to find more suitable employers. Planters so often forget the importance of pride and many a cane fire is the result of an insensitive dismissal. So you see, I am not all

11

altruism. I have my interests to guard. They are my pre-occupation.

I point to the monkeys on the back of the Land Rover. The induna calls one of the cutters. The man, a wiry Pondo, thanks me and removes the carcasses. Pondos relish monkey meat whereas Zulus regard the animal as unclean. I return to the Land Rover. As I head back to the yard a column of ochre dust sprays out behind the vehicle like aerosol paint gilding the foliage and drying the leaves, contorting them. On past the dam with its clotted sluice where some of the stream escapes to continue to the Tugela and out to sea. Past the bank where the kingfishers nest, the lower holes deserted after leguaan raids, and into an avenue of young planes.

I often wonder whether I will see these trees in their prime. It is a question every thinking person here must ask himself. One never knows in this part of the world. Things are so volatile in Africa: banned movements undermine covertly for years and governments fall overnight. A visa is suddenly needed to travel there. Certain passport holders are no longer welcome and holiday cottages are abandoned. Faithful servants are paid a remittance to look after them in the vague hope that one day things will return to what they were. They never do. Our capacity for deception is vast. Mozambique, Angola, Rhodesia — what was such fun last year no longer exists.

This farm has been in the family for four generations which is long for Natal. What was once a growing community is now a pale finger clasped by KwaZulu. The Zulus demand consolidation and expropriation is a constant bogey. I am tempted at low ebbs to exploit rather than nourish — to cut back on fertiliser, not to maintain the roads — but, despite the increasing frequency of arson in the cane, my bourgeois caution intrudes. Continuity has its own momentum which even the Bambata Rebellion failed to halt. Down there, where I have just shot the monkeys, a white civil servant was disembowelled by the rebels. Over that hill stands a cairn in memory of a skirmish. The colonial troops used their Maxims to deadly effect: sixty-four of the rebels were killed for the loss of one trooper. Surely those were as troubled times? And yet we are still here. My fear of being labelled the timid link impels me to press on.

The ephemeral quality of these surroundings is my inspiration. What is tumbling pell-mell can be caught, like Harry's experiences, on paper. I will deposit this tale somewhere for others later to discover. Publication is not imperative; only the knowledge that hidden somewhere, in an asbestos cylinder, is a record of what is now. Then, no matter what, things here will continue. I am already beginning to think of a suitable hiding place.

Beyond the saplings lies the expanse of cane which so characterises this eastern seaboard. Millions of stalks among millions of leaves. Forever restless, the fields emit a low hum which can be heard by those blessed with acuteness. It is a collective sound, like the response of a crowd, which is greater than the sum of its parts. Sarah's voice is part of it, as are other messages. Consequently I have come to need the reassurance of this therapeutic hum while not always consciously hearing it. Should it suddenly cease, the silence would be deafening. This dependence appears ironic when my livelihood is the systematic razing of fields. But I console myself that my presence is necessary; without me the cycle would continue but rankness would intrude. Uncut cane will arrow and go to seed. Gentle culling is essential to provide the golden eggs. Years of privileged educations and generous dowries have made it a fine art. Our exploitation is of the subtlest kind. Like true hunters we also nurture. As long as there is a future it pays us to.

Subtlety is imperative. In this melting pot so much is at stake. I have enough enemies not to want to foster more. Being implantations, like the cane, we flourish but must accept our limitations. Those millions of stalks are bursting with sap yet they are infertile. Imported cultivars, like some animals in a zoo, lack the incentive to continue. With us everything is for the short term. Things will see us out but not the children. Under hot-house conditions the experiment station develops seed cane. Alternatively we cut stalks and plant them in furrows. There being no natural births, these fields are brimming with clones and test-tube babies. Such are the concessions.

13

All this has crystallised over the last few years. So often one lives in the midst of something without understanding it. My childhood on the farm was markedly lacking in any real knowledge of its workings. Only after the death in action of my elder brother Michael during one of our army's forays into Angola was I summoned home from university in Ireland. Apolitical, he had the misfortune, like so many others, of being in the wrong place at the wrong time. Neither did he love the system nor hate the enemy. I am reminded of that couplet from Yeats's poem on the death of Major Robert Gregory:

> Those that I fight I do not hate,
> Those that I guard I do not love.

And so I abandoned academia for the mechanics of cane cultivation. I am undecided whether it was preordained. Let it suffice to say that with one link in the hereditary chain broken, it was imperative to couple on its successor.

Back in the yard, my brogues pad towards the Indian mechanic. Looking down at them, I feel strangely detached; like a floating head observing two leather objects tilling the dust. Two miniature dust clouds escort me towards the sparks which are splattering from the welder into the hibiscus hedge. The mechanic lifts his visor; the trailer will be ready tomorrow. I instruct a Pondo to wash the back of the Land Rover clean of monkey blood.

The yard has always been an important point of convergence. Everything seems linked to it like spokes to a hub. It was, and still is, merely a square of bare earth towered over by gums and flanked by white-washed sheds, a hibiscus hedge shielding the chicken-run and stables, and its entrance, a gravel road which bears left and funnels into the avenue of planes. Years of punishment from tractors and trailers and regular dousings with old sump oil have compacted the surface of the thoroughfare to near concrete. Only the crawler makes an impression, leaving its delicate twin ladders down the channel between the parade of trailers and the roller and

14

grader which squat patiently beside the sheds. Then, another day's pounding obliterates *its* tracery.

It was here that every morning during those endless preschool days I criss-crossed my present steps, tricycling slowly between the sheds, stopping at the stables to snoop through the milking stalls and day-old-chick batteries before moving on, via the yard, to the workshop to pester the then mechanic with requests while he stripped a tractor or welded something together. It was always warm and bats hung in dark clusters from the gums where the bees were busy. The geese, waddling out from behind the rotavator, gaggled like Mother: 'James you must wear sandals or you'll get the sandworm.' Always the sandworm. Ingwe came from the stables with the milk in two silver buckets with scratches on their sides. We talked in Zulu and I stuck my fingers into the warm frothiness and licked them. The mill hooter tooted softly. The cane whispered in the distance and Father came from it with his stick and khakis and Mother called like the mosque Indian.

Each weekday evening all the remaining loaded trailers were parked along the hedge to await delivery to the mill first thing in the morning. From them I plucked stalks with long internodes and, with a deftness long since lost, peeled off the hard skins and chewed the crisp pith. The pulpy gobbets in the dust made my progress a cinch to follow as I cycled onwards like a scuttling insect through the echoing innards of a pot pourri jar, drunk with its sounds and smells.

The lunch bell clangs.

A possible hiding place for my manuscript cylinder has just occurred to me. In the cellar, behind the racks of pinotage and riesling, is a mossy fissure whose mouth resembles a tired vulva. Perhaps a psychiatrist will search the smouldering ruin. If nothing else, the symbolism of his find may intrigue him.

2

This bungalow's style has its origin in displacement; like many others in the tropics and sub-tropics, it was built by a colonial. Its white walls, high ceilings and deep verandas bear witness to a horror of heat. My father added shutters, ostensibly for greater coolness and privacy but, on reflection, I suspect that security was his real motive. Simple calculation places them just after Sharpeville; things aren't what they used to be and all that. It now has the appearance of lived-in decay. What was once perhaps a blot on the landscape has, through the years, established a certain harmony with its surroundings. The garden, no longer manicured, is an effusion of indigenous and exotic vegetation and the huge flat-crown off the sitting-room provides added shade from beyond the reach of its roots. Everything seems to combine visibly, projecting inwards towards the bungalow; only the front lawn rebels, pulling one's attention away towards the gully and on beyond the valley to the sea. Surrounding sounds advance on the centre in diminishing circles: the profusion of bird calls; the moaning of palm fronds; the singing of black women; the barking of bushbuck; the sighing of the cane: from time to time all these and more home in on me from outside.

The lunchtime news on the radio is depressing as usual and I can't help wallowing in it as I move through to my bedroom for my afternoon nap. The world seems full of squabbles. Altruistic compromise is absent in the warring. Subversion is rife: arsonists move nightly through the cane. I hold my pale banner aloft, declaring my determination to defend my estate. But, and I see immediately the implication of my stand, I have become one of those who refuse to compromise, one of those whom I despise. How difficult it is to take a completely justified stand when most claims have a degree of legitimacy. Perspective is crucial: hence the inevitable

16

problem of what is which; is the arsonist a terrorist or freedom fighter? Giving often means losing but resilience means a lessening of the chances of breakage. Paradoxically, I realise that one has to change to remain the same. And yet in changing one can never be the same again, but ultimately more the same than if one does not change and a break takes place. It is all frighteningly fluid yet the fluidity is frighteningly necessary. But how much change? That is the question.

My bed is warm. I close the shutters and lie down in the gloom. I consider reading further in one of the books on my bedside table — Roy Campbell, two local histories and Honwana — but decide instead just to lie in the twilight. A mower drones on the front lawn and tractors murmur in the distance, stitching together the mill and the fields with the dusty threads of their wakes. Beyond them sighs the delicate lullaby of the cane: a swishing sleepy sound. The room smells of gun oil; regular cleanings of my Holland & Holland have left behind that special fragrance which takes me back decades. I can almost hear my father's voice intoning the golden rules of gunmanship.

On my dressing table, captured by a lens's blink, stands Sarah. I managed to coax the now ochre and mottled photograph from a distant relative on the pretext that I was a dabbler in genealogy. After a protracted rally of letters she arrived and I was confronted by her person. Pictured early in widowhood, her appearance is suitably sombre. Her features are unmistakably patrician: a conventionally beautiful face elongated into a resemblance of Virginia Woolf. Her fragility is disturbing, suggesting a latent hysteria. At her feet is a beagle with its head on its front paws, giving the photograph the air of a brass rubbing.

It is still difficult to link this faded cardboard with the voice from the cane. I used to study the photograph as she spoke but I have recently been weaned of that. Each time I see it, the old mystery is revived: why was I of all people chosen for this dialogue? Never having toyed with spiritualism or used the Ouija board, I have none of the credentials. Perhaps my need for the cane's hum singled me out. Perhaps, like many metaphysical riddles, there is no answer. As yet I have detected no central message in the campaign experiences of her lamented soldier husband. Why they aren't now united also remains a mystery but let it suffice at this stage to say that for some reason or other, or no reason, I was chosen and my curiosity leads me on.

I have gleaned something of Harry from my collection of Africana books. The usual tomes on the Zulu War merely mention his name occasionally but *The Zululand Campaign of 1879* by Madbolt and Shannon, which I picked up second-hand in Dublin while at university there, is a trove of information. A memorial volume to those British officers who lost their lives in the war, it has both a cabinet photograph and a two-page memoir on Harold Arthur Colville. A younger son of Sir Alfred Lewis Colville, Bart., of Corsehill, Co. Galway, he was educated at Charterhouse and Sandhurst. After receiving a commission in the 24th Regiment (2nd Warwickshire), he served briefly in Gibraltar before proceeding to the Cape for the Ngqika and Gcaleka Campaign. This was followed by a sojourn in Ceylon — where, of course, the union was made — until the outbreak of the Zulu War.

The oval cabinet photograph reveals a presentable young man resplendent in full-dress uniform and sporting the wispy moustache beloved of subalterns. It is quite an ordinary face, radiating the usual self-confidence of privilege with a suggestion of twittishness. But I must check myself; my affection for Sarah often makes me hypercritical. In fact there is a facial similarity between the spouses: both have finely formed bridges to their noses and expressions of aloofness. Each looking for him- or herself in the other, and all that. I find, however, that Sarah's sombre clothing and obvious grief instil in her an element of tragedy which is ennobling whereas Harry has an air of arrogance.

Moses serves afternoon tea at four o'clock as he has done for as long as I can remember. Pure Ceylon tea with a plate of sultana-studded rock-cakes. I often wonder whether some of what I am drinking comes from the Matale District. Perhaps this murky liquid has its origin in a glossy arbour beyond the coolie lines. A young couple; bared petticoats and gently perspiring softness.

18

Life on isolated farms needs ritual. Like many other colonials, my grandparents set themselves standards which they maintained assiduously. One of these involved bathing and dressing for dinner. Shortly before six o'clock each evening, they emerged from their rooms — she in a long dress, wearing a string of pearls, and he in dark trousers and a white shirt — and settled down for a sundowner on the veranda. After they had listened to the radio news, he would read a pot-boiler while she played patience. At precisely seven o'clock the gong would sound and they would retire indoors for dinner. Usually, as they were poised on the threshold, the mill hooter informed them from far below in the valley that all was on schedule. Like clockwork, the mill and house on the hill were linked, with the radio news providing another ballast. Unlike our broadcasts today, theirs were a reassurance.

My grandmother once explained to me the importance of this routine: isolation surreptitiously erodes that veneer of civilisation which is essential. Without it we would descend into slovenliness. I was secretly derisive at the time but now know better.

My parents also habitually bathed and dressed for dinner, although less formally, and replaced the sets of Wagner records which were my grandparents' favourite with Mantovani. For weeks afterwards the lean-to near the stables resounded to grand Teutonic strains as the servants, having salvaged the brittle discs from the rubbish bin, subjected themselves to the strange music of the abelungu. I too have inherited the routine: I shower at dusk but dress less formally still in a clean pair of my usual khaki trousers and a white shirt. As a further gesture I add a cravat during Andrea's visits. From her *haute couture* perspective the combination apparently appears quaint and intriguing.

Despite our years of intimacy, she chides me for being an enigma, a role which I foster. I don't know whether my masks (if they are that) are masks. Whatever they are, they keep her guessing. Should my pith be revealed, I am uncertain whether it would sustain her. Revelation alone would resolve my doubt but with things as they are, I am loath to take the risk. That is if there is one. I have frequently been told to remove a

19

mask and be myself and yet I have never been aware of playing the supposed charade. Masks, if they consciously exist, are so much part of us that I wonder whether they mask anything. Perhaps we are merely husks which reflect our situation. What Andrea sees may be what she wants to see or a pretence to balk my next offensive. Our relationship thrives on tension.

After tea I set out on my last rounds for the day. My routine seldom changes: first to the sheds and stables, then to the cutting to count the stacks due for carting the following day, and then home, via a circuit through the garden, for a shower. For the sake of fitness and, indirectly, vanity, I insist on walking, ignoring the lure of the Land Rover. Recently I have been taking the Holland & Holland with me, chiefly in the hope that I may catch red-handed a monkey raiding party, but increasingly for self-defence. In addition to the arson, robberies and assaults are on the increase. In the long dusk shadows one can so easily be caught unawares. I frequently ask myself whether I am being alarmist. Do the hardened, skin-cancered planters feel the same insecurities or am I just a misplaced bibliophile ill-suited to the harsh realities of this frontier existence? I am haunted by over-reaction, knowing the great effectiveness of understatement. Am I over-reacting? What do you who have unearthed this manuscript think? The dividing line is painfully narrow. On the one hand is foolhardy casualness, countered on the other by obsessive security which provokes ridicule from the black labourers. They scoff at timidity so deception is essential. They must think that I am merely on the look-out for monkeys which, while partly true, obscures my other, darker, motive.

I remember Father being called out by the nightwatchman to adjudicate, like Solomon, in labour disturbances. The simmering deputation would be waiting outside the kitchen and, dressed in his paisley dressing-gown, he would attempt to reconcile the combatants, often a Pondo and a Zulu. Each would have to relate his story while the induna stood between them like a referee. Sometimes scuffles would break out and handcuffs were used. Apparently undeterred, Father would be in their midst, his hands in his pockets, as he reached a verdict. Years later he confided to me that nestled in his right palm was a .32 revolver. Fortunately he never had need to use it. His reputation for compassion and justice spread throughout the district untainted by the knowledge that he felt a need to arm himself.

And so appearances are crucial. Not only must he be fearless, but the nkosaan must be seen regularly. Overseeing maintains that tension which is productive. Reprimands are seldom necessary but the planter must create the illusion of omnipresence; cutters will be confronted by him from behind a stack, shotgun reports will echo up the valley and the Land Rover's dusty wake will hang poised above the stalk tips. Indunas and sirdars reinforce this tension but they too need spot checks. On my return after a day or two ill in bed I can feel the deterioration.

As it is after five, the sheds and yard are deserted. The row of recently returned tractors emits snapping sounds as the corrugated iron roof does in the evening after a hot day. Rats scoot along the rafters. After inspecting the repaired trailer, I pass the stables where the cows are being milked — clanging buckets and the incessant bleating of a weaning calf. Under this pine is where Ingwe used to slaughter the chickens. Holding each like a bagpipe under his elbow, he bent back their heads, sawing at their necks with his penknife. Blood splattered through the feathers and decorated the exposed roots. Morbidly transfixed, I was a hovering witness to the spectacle. At night, said Ingwe, he had seen wild cats licking the patterns.

Several years later Michael and I spent a holiday with a school friend who lived on a ranch in Swaziland. Our host, wanting to verify his dormitory stories, escorted us proudly to the abattoir. Scores of lowing oxen were milling about in a kraal. Positioning ourselves near what looked like a spray-race, we watched as ox after ox was forced into the narrow passage and shot point-blank in the forehead. As each collapsed, kicking, a chain was fastened to its back hooves and it was suspended from a rail. As each carcass progressed down the production line, it was drained of blood, skinned and systematically prepared for refrigeration. Like a dwarfish

21

ghoul I followed my older companions between the drums of blood. Unable to erase the memory, I suffered from a prolonged succession of nightmares in which that distant ranch and this tree remained grisly associates. Subsequent visits to Swaziland's holiday valley have been tainted and the roulette wheels and blue films roll to a bellowing backdrop.

At the cutting I count nine stacks. They will all be at the mill tomorrow morning. Several late cutters pass me on their way back to the compound. Have I shot a monkey? a Pondo enquires decorously. I shake my head.

Each cutter has a daily task. No working hours are imposed but the majority prefer an early start so as to be finished by noon. To escape the midsummer heat, several cut by moonlight. Sometimes, during Sarah's visits, we hear their singing across the valley. It pleases her; Harry had apparently mentioned how beautifully the locals sing.

Several hadedas wing their way to the umdonis in the gully, their raucous cries gyring across the cane fields as a late tractor and trailer return from the mill. They bounce past on the dirt road and the goggled driver raises a hand in salute. I can hear the alternate accelerating and braking long after the jangling tandem has disappeared in the cane.

3

I sit on the veranda as the night settles, listening to the breeze disturb the palms whose fronds scissor like heron wings. The lights of the sugar mill and company houses pop on in the distant cane and beyond them waits the darkness of KwaZulu. On clear nights, using binoculars, I can pick out the occasional glow of a brazier and the sweep of car headlights which resemble slow-motion tracer. The crickets begin their shrilling, minutely vibrating the grass blades. Bats zigzag into the shadows. Below the lawn the cane hushes softly. Relaxed from my shower and several whiskies, I scan the slope of cane, palms, amatungulu and wild bananas and, in the distance, the hump of bush before the dunes and the metamorphosis on the horizon: a coaster discarding its dark hull for rows of twinkling lights and edging southwards into the crescent of palms. I pour another J&B — the siphon gargles — and imagine the pounding sea, orchestrating with it the sounds of the palms, amatungulu and bananas and the barks of bushbuck from deeper in the undergrowth. I combine the delicate rhythms on my flute, playing Bach and Handel in time with the night.

The phone rings and I ease myself out of my wicker chair and enter the hall. The exchange's gutteral mumblings '. . . hold on for Jo'burg.'

'Hello?'

It's Andrea. Her last assignment is at nine on Friday morning. She will be flying down. Can she spend the weekend?

'Yes.'

I begin playing, drowning the darkness in the richness of its pattern. I turn towards the flatcrown and see the twin glowing beads among the branches. I play on, my fingers tripping along the silverness of the flute. Presently the beads descend and move within reach of the light sifting through the shutters. The bushbaby rises up slowly on its hindlegs and flicks its bushy tail, watching me steadfastly with huge amazed eyes. For a few seconds we are locked in a staring game, then it begins to dance, keeping its eyes fixed on my moving fingers. It steps and shuffles on the lawn, stops, then suddenly drops onto all fours and scampers away. Back in the flatcrown it peers down at me, its eyes glowing.

With the dance over, Sarah must be nearing. I raise my crystal tumbler and through it watch a torch bobbing near the stables, moving up past the sheds and across the lawn, snapping off in the shadows.

'Yes Shezi?'

'A fire nkosaan, over near the main road.'

I follow him around the house towards the avenue. An orange glow is visible through the matting of branches.

'Is it this side of the boundary?'

'Yes nkosaan.'

I instruct him to alert the induna, tractor drivers and the men in the compound. I will meet them there. Brutus joins me and I lower the back flap of the Land Rover for him.

As I turn onto the wider district road, the fire can be heard above the sound of the engine. An entire field appears to be alight and a brisk breeze is driving the fire down the hillside towards the watercourse with its flanking bush. Plaits of flame spiral upwards and outwards, rocketing bundles of burning trash and nests in their updraught. Although most of these incendiaries extinguish before they descend over another field, some get through and widen our front. I run down a break with the heat smarting my face. Trailer loads of cutters are arriving and I must choose the point for the back-burn. Tongues of flame lick ravenously from leaf to leaf, causing the stalks to ooze and pop like braai-ing sausages. A cane rat bullets past me. After assessing the speed of the fire and the time needed to cut the break, I decide on a point not far from the watercourse. Being seasoned cutters, they know the drill. The induna barks commands and they begin slashing at the stalks, scything along the contour. Following them, I use my lighter to set the back-burn. From within, the sound of the fire is deafening: a crackling roar like the sustained blast of an ambush.

24

All animals are frightened by fire but my fear runs deeper. While a cane rat scampers frantically away from the immediate danger, I am haunted by other associations. Confronted by a sheet of flame and its accompanying din, I am always drawn back to my childhood in the early sixties. Night after night, for months on end, when that season of subversion was at its peak, I remember standing in my pyjamas at the sitting-room window as the scattered blazes advanced through the darkness. The widespread destruction outside created a tension which was felt even by Michael and me. Braced for the blow, Father waited for the nightwatchman's summons or the tele-phone call from a neighbour requesting assistance.

On some nights, especially when the wind was high, there were five or more fires. Consequently dry windy eve-nings are even now loaded with menace. In August, before the spring rains, when the cane is tinder and the hot dry wind rasps down from the Drakensberg, I put myself on alert. Forcing myself not to tipple as much as usual, I wait on the veranda as farms in the distance bordering KwaZulu begin to glow. Tonight my restraint has paid off; the few tots have given me that lucidity which precedes clouding.

As the back-burn establishes itself and steadies, it is met at points by the renegade. Briefly the intensity doubles and then like a climax subsides.

Back at the Land Rover, I use its roof as a vantage point, watching the cutters emerge along the boundary avenue as the fire closes behind them. We seem to have caught this one in time as nowhere along its length has the back-burn been breached. Cutters are emerging from the darkness near the watercourse, their faces sheened with sweat. We exchange greetings and their teeth glint in the half-light. They seem animated and cheerful. The fire has been beaten but I instruct a group to remain behind to scour the field for glowing embers. Perhaps it was started by accident — usually a cigar-ette butt thrown carelessly out of a passing car — although that is unlikely. Many planters deceive themselves that this is the cause or, at worst, concede that an idle cutter may have turned arsonist because burnt cane, being unencumbered with trash, is easier to cut. But there have been too many

25

fires this season to discount arson. Why, one may ask, does anybody want to set fields alight? The honest answer is simple: as in the early sixties, systematic arson is part of an elaborate process of destabilisation. Alarm undermines. Cane is destroyed or its sucrose content is reduced. Routines are disrupted as neighbours must help to get the burnt cane milled before it rots. Wives are assaulted while their husbands are out fighting the fires. Gradually the veneer of peaceful affluence begins to crack.

In the long term my cutters have nothing to lose. I am the loser. And yet they rise enthusiastically to the challenge; the fire must be beaten. Their faces reflect the satisfaction of a job well done. It is at moments like this that I realise how much I admire them. But, things being what they are here, I must qualify my statement before I am drowned by yells of *kaffirboetie* or *patroniser*. Simply, without either bravado or magnanimity, I admire them. Perhaps it is I who is making the fuss but it is strange how controversial such a simple statement has become.

A coucal calls liquidly from near the watercourse. Brutus snuffles out from the charred stalks and I lift him onto the back. Easing the Land Rover up the rutted break, I follow a trailer-load of cutters onto the narrow private road. Like a team returning victorious from an away game, they are laughing and singing. At the avenue they turn right towards the compound in the valley and I continue to the house. The sound of their singing recedes into the cane.

Although it is late, Moses has stayed on and he serves my dinner of steak and kidney pie and imfino. I have loved the latter since childhood when, like the black women, I picked it between rows of cane. A half-bottle of Cape riesling was a summer routine which is now perennial. Wisps of ash from the fire cling to my khakis. Any attempt to remove them is futile as they powder on touch. The china blackbird, looking more like an Indian mynah, gawks at me from within its ruff of pastry. Coffee is served in the sitting-room and I grill Moses about the fire. Does he think it was an accident?

No, he feels it was deliberate. But he would have heard if it was one of us. There has been talk of smooth outsiders in

26

the district. It is not, he assures me, my fault; there are other, bigger, things. There is a growing restlessness. He has heard talk of trouble in other areas.

'But don't the police keep a check on these things?'

It is not, he replies, like before when my father had troubles. Then there were informers. Now things are different. The people are frightened to talk. There are too many threats.

'But what do I do?' I implore him, 'I can't just wait until everything is burnt.'

No, he knows a sangoma who will help. She sees what we cannot see. There is nothing she doesn't know. Once she has told me, I must let it be known that I know. The people will then be wary of me. They are frightened of the spirits. Not even the outsiders will change their minds. But he will tell me when I can visit the sangoma.

'Thank you Moses.'

The same person who had played Black Peter with me so long ago when I couldn't sleep withdraws and I can hear him washing dishes until the back door taps shut. Then, as he has done for decades, I assume he walks down the avenue to his room behind the stables. Besides Sarah and Andrea, he is my only confidant. Perhaps more than anyone, he can monitor the pulse of the farm. On the infrequent nights that I spend away, I entrust everything to him. He maintains the house, feeds Brutus, chivvies the gardeners, and more than any induna keeps things going. In many ways he is my mentor. Should he leave, it would be difficult for me to continue. Without his counsel I would be out of touch with the workings. A solitary white in a big house on the hill cannot, despite his familiarity with his surroundings, know everything about his labour force which, in such a labour-intensive enterprise as sugar farming, is essential.

But why, you may ask, should he confide in me? I have pondered on this for years. As you know, I regard them as the ultimate winners. What use is collaboration with the loser? The answer, I think, is that he actually sees himself as my mentor. Having lived his entire life on the farm and seen it from both sides, he seems to be that rarity, a true moderate.

While supporting the aspirations of his people, he seems also to have an admiration for the order and tranquillity of our particular status quo which he is loath to see destroyed. I suppose I am a benign dictator and he fears the alternatives. Being mission educated, he has a horror of covetousness. I tend to agree with him but my perspective is undermined by my privilege. I can afford to be idealistic and yet I hope I have no illusions. I can appreciate his reassurances but I see their limitations. One has only to remember the lot of the loyal house servants during the MauMau. Like Moses they were moderate, but so often moderation is swamped by a mass response.

My study is the logical progression of my father's whose it once was. My school and university photographs replace his on the same hooks and his already brimming bookshelves have been further burdened by my collection. As another gesture to continuity I have hung side-by-side two photographs of our old school's main block, taken during our respective attendances. Despite the interim of thirty years, the changes are merely cosmetic. Is this a valid touchstone? Only time will tell whether I am right or not. I envy you your perspective. Yet you too must look to your successors for the significance of your actions. Did you find this asbestos cylinder amidst smouldering ruins or in the cellar of an old, peaceful bungalow? That is the question that haunts me.

I move to the window and peer out between the open shutters. The garden lights (another security feature in an aesthetic disguise) illuminate patches of the ordered chaos, but the gully and the valley beyond are lost in darkness. Monkey chatter bursts like distant rifle fire. It is too late for my serenade and meeting with Sarah. Also, I lack the necessary calmness. It will have to be postponed. I repeat the cancellation to myself, hoping that by some telepathic means she will understand. The fire has intruded and, although defeated, it has taken its toll. I need a whisky and cheroot. A coucal calls from the foot of the lawn.

I pour a J&B and lean back in my leather chair as the first heavy drops patter onto the corrugated iron roof. Presently the rain increases and I switch off the light and sit drinking in the dark, listening to the rush outside. It falls in torrents, splattering over the veranda and pinking in a fine mist between the shutters. In the distance I hear the tractor returning with the remaining cutters, the downpour having completed their task. Brutus snuffles outside and I let him in. He has that characteristic wet-dog smell. Whenever I draw on my cheroot I glimpse his wrinkled profile in the glass of a team photograph. He farts and then there is nothing but the sound of the rain. Closing my eyes, I slump back into my chair. Repeating my apology to Sarah, I sink into sleep.

At dawn I emerge to find a fine drizzle falling. The rain, it seems, has undergone a purgation: the previous night's torrent is now a slanting veil of tranquil sound. Slicing softly downwards.

4

Stuck. The heavily loaded trailer is up to its axle in the mud
at the bottom of the cut field, only yards from the reeds
and umdonis which hug the watercourse. With the night's
downpour, the earth has jellied and I feel its dark tackiness
as I circle the trailer, pondering on how it should be extri-
cated. A re-emergence of the drizzle causes the cutters to pull
the hoods of their yellow raincoats up over their heads, giving
them the strange appearance of black-stamened lilies. I beckon
to the three Indian drivers and they walk across the trash to
me.

'Pillay, take your tractor and hook it up to the trailer.
Moonsamy, put yourself in front of Pillay's tractor and tow
him with the cable. Naidoo, take the crawler and face it up
the slope above the trailer. Fix a cable and just keep it tight
while the others are towing. We don't want the trailer to tip
over in the mud. Move very slowly and let the others do the
main pulling.'

They return to their vehicles, start them, and begin to
position themselves while the induna instructs the cutters to
secure the cables. I light a cheroot and draw deeply on it. I
sniff the air, breathing the warm humus and the sweetness of
rotting figs and the cane stumps. Sarah wafts across to me and
I fill my lungs with her. The mud between the trailer and the
stream is pocked with wild pig hoof-prints. Acned with
them. It amazes me how the pigs can live in the fields without
ever being seen. Only heard occasionally. There is something
about their elusiveness: a Circean mischief, a talisman, an
engraving of cloven ju-ju beside the watercourses.

'Ready master,' one of the drivers calls out above the
gargling of the engines. I wave the cutters away from the
cables and signal. Both tractors and the crawler roar and the
cables tighten with a series of staccato cracks. The trailer
rocks reluctantly as both tractors see-saw in the muddy cane

trash, their back wheels spinning like catherine-wheels, spraying out showers of mud. The crawler inches up the hillside at right angles to the tractors and trailer and its frayed cable cracks and twists with the strain. Blue-grey exhaust fumes chimney into the drizzle and drift towards the monkeys which have appeared in the umdonis above the stream. As insolent as ever, they chatter among the leaves, craning their necks and watching Brutus who scampers about beneath the trees, barking. The trailer stubbornly refuses to budge. I signal and the drivers decelerate. I turn to the induna and address him in Zulu.

'Get the men to put trash under the tractors' wheels.'

The monkeys' chattering is audible above the idling engines. I signal. The tractors and crawler strain forward and the trailer rocks on its haunches before rising slowly out of the hollow, teetering briefly, then snailing forward onto more solid ground. I count the monkeys: thirty-nine heads but more likely triple that number tucked away in the foliage.

While several cutters remove the cables, I cross to the induna for the attendance record. Four men are resting, more than usual, but obviously last night's fire-fighting and the drizzle have played their part. Now that these last loads are on their way to the mill, we can start carting the burnt cane which one gang has already been allocated to cut. The rich dark soil is spongy underfoot. Hopefully this rain will keep the arsonists at bay and tide us over until the summer storms begin. I burp: kippers, then walk back to the Land Rover. The drizzle midge-patters softly on the windscreen and the sound of the engines silences the monkeys. Perhaps it reminds them of other sounds. I picture them tensed for the burst and sniff-sniffing, half expecting to smell cordite. Letting the engine idle, I light another cheroot and sit smoking in the misting cab as the convoy passes: two tractors, one towing the recalcitrant load, and the crawler whose tracks jingle.

All the drivers on the farm are Indians. Unlike their ancestors who were imported from India to work as indentured labourers for the sugar industry, most of those who have remained on the farms are now artisans, drivers or sirdars. The local black men, who initially refused to work as cutters, now fill those jobs. This subservient position, coupled with the exploitation of unsophisticated blacks by some Indian traders, has fanned the existing antagonism between the races. Although an uneasy peace continues, there is one fact which cannot be ignored: like us whites, the Indians are implantations. Like us, they have adopted, not inherited, this soil. But like the house sparrow and mynah, we have both adapted. Generations have come and gone who have known nothing else but this landscape. Like the immigrant birds we now deserve inclusion in manuals of indigenous species but, being importations, we cannot avoid the tension between us and our environment. Only time can bring about the eventual miscegenation when colour genes alone will scuffle for dominance until their distribution is uniform.

Both the Indians and us so-called liberal whites are faced with the same predicament. Caught between the Afrikaner nationalist hegemony and the rise of black consciousness, we can only wait at the ropes and hope not to be injured while the contestants wrestle. Unfortunately, as in a tag-team bout, it is inevitable that we will be dragged into the mêlée.

Being emasculated minorities, we vacillate between support for the regime and the liberation movements. Trapped by the urgency of our indecision, we accumulate wealth while the going's good. Gradually this greed becomes hysterical and only those with sufficient acuity can arrest their deterioration. The remainder, finding the tension intolerable, either leave the country or continue until the paralysis sets in. As the centre softens, so we undermine our own resistance. I can see it so clearly now but in seconds it will be clouded again.

The monkeys are retreating downstream, skittling the tree-tops. An animated Brutus scampers after them. Despite the sodden earth and falling drizzle, I stub the remains of my cheroot into the ashtray rather than toss it out of the window; an environmental conditioning which I barely notice. Fires, like snakes, are dangerous. Never throw a match or stompie onto the ground. Likewise, keep an eye on the undergrowth for any fluid curve or sudden movement. No longer do we merely have temperate adders to contend with. Mambas, cobras and our adders are in a different league. Consequently, we have had to adapt.

The stark, charred stalks resemble thousands of spears stuck shaft-end into the ground by a retreating impi. I juggle with the metaphor: is it a mere ploy or a real retreat? Have they been beaten or are they amassing elsewhere? But, as I learnt during my national service, their retreat is always a rout whereas ours is merely a retrograde action. Such is the crap that we are taught. Is this small field of burnt cane, now being cut and carted to the mill, not a pyrrhic victory? They burnt my cane but their arson attempt wasn't a success. I am now on their trail. I am attacking in defence but will I win in the end? Yes, says the district, but I am not so sure.

A tractor and trailer bounces across the plough furrows and winches on a load. I summon the induna. Because of the rain, the men can take the remainder of the day off once they have cut the last few rows.

Driving back along the boundary, I pass through a dell of arum lilies near the previous Indian settlement. The remains of the clapboard cottages appear among the weeds on the hillside. Last year, on a pretext of greater efficiency but essentially for security reasons, I moved the Indian families to new brick buildings near the yard. Despite their pleas for renovations instead, I insisted on the move, knowing that they would eventually understand. I intend to plough up all the wasted land for cane, leaving only the avocado and mango trees, but feel reluctant to give the instruction, assuming that this spot is somehow hallowed. Three generations and the worship of their gods must have instilled in it an eastern character. Its own colours, smells and sounds announced its peculiarity. And yet all this may merely be my attempt to preserve vestiges from my past. Perhaps the Indians disliked the location despite their initial reluctance to move. Perhaps, in the relative luxury of their new homes, they have forgotten the importance of their previous world. I must remind myself that I wooed them into the laager. That was my wish, as is the utilisation of all available land for cane. Therefore the instructions must be given despite my own attempts to preserve what has already gone.

33

Down there stood the pooja house, like a blue corrugated iron privy festooned with golden shower and jade vine, and hung with bobbing trinkets which tinkled incessantly. Flanking the doorway was an assortment of vases which, as a child, I believed, or perhaps dreamed, contained human ashes. The memory probably stems from a photograph: white robed figures bathing in the Ganges, and funeral pyres; perhaps tucked away among the avocados and mangoes, down there by the stream. Several colourful flags on tall bamboo poles fluttered above the intricately carved gables and the door had tacked on it a strange portrait of some bright-eyed goddess, painted in colours of a different, eastern, lustre — so foreign to home with its cool pastels and cooler whites. From my vantage point in the cleft of a rubber tree, the portrait resembled a reddish dab on the face of the door. Only closer inspection revealed the colour spectrum.

For hours at a time I watched as the Indian women, swathed in their saris, vanished behind that door with its divine face. As the door closed behind each woman, I teetered among the branches, feverishly excited, convinced that strange kaleidoscopic rites were being performed in the darkness of the privy. Throughout the day they arrived, appearing from the cane, gliding through the mangoes and avocados, easing themselves around my trunk and disappearing into the darkness behind that face. While one woman was about her privy business, the others sat in groups beneath the mangoes and their voices sifted across to me: feminine eastern sounds fading into the tinkling trinkets. Exotic mynah profiles in the grass.

About every quarter of an hour a woman emerged from the darkness and slipped serenely past my rubber tree, dissolving into the yellow and green montage of the mangoes. Then another woman would detach herself from a group and ease her delicate form into the darkness, only to emerge later and vanish into the trees amidst the sound of distant voices and tinkling trinkets.

What, I implored myself, happened in that darkness? What were the women doing behind that door? What happened in those privy parts? Who lured them?

34

I never learned the answers. And now that the pooja house has gone no amount of dithering will revive it. Only this chronicle has some of that ability.

As I have given everyone the afternoon off, there is nothing for me to supervise so at lunch I down a bottle of pinotage as a libation to the rainbird and whoever. En route to my bedroom for my siesta my movements again feel detached — I am a brain and this is a body obeying me. Each footfall on the Persian runner is at my command. I am omnipotent. I order this body to lie down on the bed and it responds. The soft sound of the rain on the roof hushes me. I am soon oblivious.

5

Through the sitting-room window I can see the drizzle. The fire crackles in the grate and over in the paddock beyond the gums the cattle stand huddled together as the drizzle whips in waves across them. I hold a crystal tumbler of J&B in both hands, enjoying its weight. The last few days of guti have broken the drought and in the distance the cane looks good and green. I have given the cutters time off again and I can see the flickering of braziers in their huts across the valley. A strange peace seems to have descended. The soaking rain means a temporary relief from fires. For some time the cane will be too wet to burn strongly. The arsonists will have to lie low.

It seems now that the elements are back on our side, but for how long? Something must be done about the arsonists. Their methods are now so much more sophisticated. Gone are the days when a ruse would scare them off. I remember what my next-door neighbour, an ex-Kenyan, had done in the sixties. He had assembled his labour force — some of whom he suspected of arson — and told them that he would shoot anyone whom he caught setting fire to his cane. He then chose a field which he intended to cut the following week. Late one night he set the field alight near its downwind edge so that it rapidly burnt itself out. He then fired three shots into the air with a shotgun before making a mound of soil topped with stones. The next day he announced that he had caught an arsonist red-handed and had shot and buried him. His grave near the boundary was a warning to others who contemplated arson. Superstition prevented anyone from tampering with the mound so its contents remained a secret and his farm was the only one in the district to escape further fires during those troubles.

His method seems ridiculous on reflection. Times have changed more than most people realise. And so have the arsonists. With outside help they have developed ingenious methods. Timing devices ensure that they are far away when the fields go up. It's no use waiting and then reacting. One has to attack in defence. Like the attempts to exterminate locusts, one has to attack their source before they spread. Ideological feelings aside, it is the only way to defend one's property.

I sink back into a deep armchair. A log in the fire wheezes and liquid drips from it and fizzles on the coals. Outside, mist has begun to scud across the window as the light fades. I light a cheroot and enjoy its stink. Brutus lies snoring on a rug in front of the fire. The front page of the newspaper announces *Mall Bomb Blast Kills Three* as its lead, with *Arms Cache Found in Durban Suburb* prominent downpage. The drizzle patters gently on the corrugated iron roof and the flames curl and lick the logs in the grate until the wigwam they'd formed collapses.

The gong gongs. Supper is kedgeree followed by biscuits and camembert with my obligatory libation. For the few years that I have been alone here on the farm, I have left culinary affairs completely to Moses. He phones through the grocery orders and the parcels are collected by one of the Indian drivers on the bi-weekly duty runs into Nonoti. Variety is limited but it suits me; my palate has been numbed by years of boarding school grub. Steak and kidney pie, rump or fillet steak (Rhodesian before the transition), Irish stew, lamb chops, kedgeree, chicken or guinea fowl, and curry complete the weekly cycle before it is repeated. Andrea balks at several dishes and instead dons an apron herself. I give Moses the evening off and he is tactfully thankful.

Tonight, immaculate in his starched whites, he has news: the sangoma can see me tomorrow. He explains the paperchase of directions and the terms of payment. A donation of money and six bottles of whisky are required before the clairvoyance. I remember with relief that I have several bottles of the cheaper shipped-out-in-bulk variety in the cellar. Squandering J&B on a tippling hag would be sacrilege.

How should I put my questions? I wonder before realising that, being a sangoma, she probably already knows my method of approach. Unlike myself, she has no doubts about the form of my future actions. Guiltily I edit my thoughts; cheaper whisky brands are equally good. My partiality is merely acquired; a mild eccentricity. But I must be specific and ask for the arsonist's name. A name is a name and the culprit should soon be in custody. I attempt to lay false trails of thought to disorientate the sangoma. She must sleuth alone.

Before he takes the coffee tray, I remind Moses that nkosazaan Andrea is expected tomorrow afternoon. The spare room must be prepared. He will, he answers softly, instruct Rose.

'Thank you Moses. Goodnight.'

'Goodnight master.'

He withdraws and for some time I can hear dishes being washed in the kitchen until the back door taps shut. The brief scrabbling of the key in the lock always heralds a feeling of loneliness but tonight it is allayed by the knowledge that tomorrow the riddle will be solved and that Andrea will be here. Before then though Sarah may emerge from the darkness for our tryst. Although I would never admit this to either, I am considerably fortified by their periodic nearness. Like a marathon runner, I last out between refreshment stops where I am rejuvenated and can continue.

Fear of some sort of accident has recently instilled in me an urgency which draws me to my desk after dinner each evening to continue this account. The gape of its chosen receptacle seems to chivvy me from behind the emptying racks and I must continue daily. So much does it occupy my thoughts that I have begun to subordinate my life to its demands. Despite my role as chronicler of my surroundings, my life now appears to be ordained by each chapter. This paper calls the tune as it were. And so I am becoming a slave to this chronicle and like a rower in a galley I am shackled to its requirements. While I am pleased with this movement towards total submersion and authenticity, I am also fearful of possible irresponsibility. Has it been ordained that this narrative will end abruptly and that I am to be offered as a sacrifice? Perhaps it has become the creator of my personal narrative

38

and I am a character dependent on its whims for my survival. Perhaps, the day before, it prescribes my actions which will in turn be captured on paper. Perhaps it is using me, like a pen, to write its story. I must ensure that it is I who is writing this chronicle and not the chronicle writing itself through me.

So much am I plagued by this dilemma that I must be certain that each experience is worthy of inclusion before I consider it. Nothing will be used merely because it happened but only because I observed it happen and wanted, through my own free will, to include it as indicative of our present predicament. I must remain superior to the experiences and choose them rather than have the era choose me as its mouth-piece. I, for reasons not fully known to myself, wish this stage in the evolution of this country to be recorded. All emphases are mine as are all omissions. It is my story. Its very personalness demands some secrecy at this stage because of the need for purity. It is my idea of now seen with an eye to the future and any judgements offered prematurely by others may reduce its purity. For better or for worse it is one man's view and must remain consistently such.

I know everyone in the district would pooh-pooh this emphasis on the future and immortality, insisting that now is now and to hell with tomorrow. Perhaps theirs is a healthy response but for me the future seems indelibly entwined with the present. Every action depends on limitations of time. All my planning is, albeit largely unconsciously, based on the assumption that at best I won't live for much more than the prescribed seventy years. Unlike the Struldbruggs we have bounds within which milestones are reached and passed. Despite the fact that I could one day be ambushed while on an evening stroll, I demand a more positive assessment: the future must be faced; stoicism rules, okay. However, should I know for certain that I am terminally ill, I would have to change my assessment completely. Being without successors, I would have to consider what would become of this thousand acres. Is there a distant relative who may appreciate it and maintain the hereditary chain. Should I give it to Andrea? Should I father a child by her in the hope that it will one day be master or mistress? Immediately the range of possibilities changes.

As it is I am plagued by how much I must put into the farm in anticipation of future crops. Occasional bouts of optimism result in new orders for fertiliser but with the horizon darkening, the sheds are now almost bare of the nourishing bags. Several cutters' huts need repairing but I have recently been postponing any additional expense, feeling that the money should instead be stashed away. Visions of a yacht or nest-egg overseas become increasingly vivid while I dither, knowing all the time that a contented labour force is a necessity. Luckily I am still astute — or compassionate — enough to see to my labourers' needs despite these niggling doubts about the worthiness of it all. I *will* have the huts repaired and I *will* order more fertiliser, at the same time aware that pessimism is rallying for further assaults.

An unsolved riddle remains: why was I chosen to be Sarah's confidant? Perhaps preordination plays a part. Admittedly I am domiciled fairly near the Zulu War battlefields, I am a descendant of Harry Colville's brother, and I have an interest in Anglo-Zulu history, but why wasn't a professor from the local university chosen or someone with more opportunity to research the exploits of her flash Harry? This question has been bothering me more recently. Also, I wonder, is there some connection between her choosing me and my writing of this account? All I can do is provide a wife's distant perspective of her husband's campaign from nearly a century later. Our communication has spanned the years and what she tells me is a combination of Harry's letters home and other information gleaned by her after his — and her — death. Perhaps her impulse is merely a precursor of mine: a desire to tell it all to future generations. Hence my desire to fuse time.

Because I am using the present tense, a strange simultaneousness has been created: my actions, my writing and your reading have all been fused so that your reading triggers off three different actions superimposed on each other. If you attain true objectivity in your reading, you will begin to appreciate our illusion and see that sleight between the lines: you-reading-about-me-writing-about-me-doing-things. Although time has elapsed between each of the experiences, by expressing them I have forced a fusion. My assumption of course is based on the fact that you will read this. Whether you can assume that your finding of this manuscript was preordained or not is yet another matter to be considered. Why should you of all people be the one to find this manuscript x years hence? Should no one find it, all will not be lost because the routine of adding to this chronicle helps in exorcising my many neuroses. As conditions worsen, so I will be made to write more through necessity.

But I must check myself as the J&B is leading me deeper into the maze. Can you see any sequence? Perhaps there isn't one and you, like the neighbours, think that I am an idiot to go on wallowing in the prospect of a gloomy future. I think too much. Only now is important. History is bunk, ghosts don't exist and if the kaffirs attack again we will mow them down. Can't you see how many new weapons we are developing? Don't you hear on the radio and television how many terrorists we are killing in South West Africa? Don't bother yourself with philosophising, it's corpses that count.

It is dark and silent in the house. Outside a faint drizzle is still falling and from the distant dam a frog chorus can just be heard. The apparent calmness makes it all that much more alarming but the knowledge that the sangoma may have something important to say tomorrow is some consolation.

6

After breakfast I hurry through my routine: consult with the indunas in my office; open the dispensary for a cutter with a nicked shin and several children with stomach troubles; and check with the mechanic about the duties of the administrative staff. With everything in a semblance of order, I set out in the Land Rover, taking the district road to the tar and then heading inland. After several kilometres the cane fields give way to the reserve with its scattered kraals and crazy-paving patches of mealies and sweet potatoes. From a white enclave into KwaZulu surrounds.

Gradually, almost pre-consciously, I become aware of a heightening of my perceptions. Casting my mind back along my recent advance, I draw a blank on the farm and district road and I now find myself absorbing the passing panorama with avidity. But why? The clarity of my observations must, I finally decide, be attributable to the following factors among other indefinable ones: my nervousness at the prospect of visiting the sangoma, the relative unfamiliarity of my surroundings (I invariably travel seawards to Nonoti and on to Durban) and, to a lesser extent, the cleanliness of the landscape in the wake of the recent rain. As in those fleeting moments, during certain evenings on the veranda (usually just prior to Sarah's arrival), I am actually noting my surroundings. Everything appears new to me and I am filled with a novice's enthusiasm. Banal scenes suddenly appear positively right. A Zulu woman and child returning from a stream with containers on their heads appear wonderfully authentic although I see similar scenes daily on the farm. Somehow, in both time and place, their actions are perfect, even ordained. Everything momentarily has an order and I enjoy one of my infrequent glimpses of its workings. The sense of well-being which it generates reminds me of my first real encounter with my surroundings when the exhilaration and afterglow were the strongest ever.

For my first three years of formal education I attended Waterbosch Farm School. Established by the sugar company for the children of its white employees, it also catered for a few of us whose parents were private planters. Throughout my attendance, those of us in the second category never constituted more than a fifth of the school's complement of twenty-five. All classes were held in a shed-like hall which doubled as the local cinema on Saturday evenings. Mother drove me the four miles to school each morning and collected me at noon. One day, through a misunderstanding, no one came to collect me. After the company bus and the cars and trucks of the other private planters had left, I waited with increasing agitation on the veranda for what must have been an hour before I decided to walk home.

Making sure that my satchel was properly closed, I set off up the wide dirt road towards the store where the farm road turned off to the left. Company drivers drove past very fast on their tractors with trailers behind them. The dust was so thick that I couldn't see for a while after they had passed. If I had been in a car with my eyes closed I would have known every bump but walking like a black was very different. Everything was around me and I had to keep looking because it was just me and the road and the cane.

The farm road was narrow and bumped down the hill to a stream and gantry. I walked on with my head bowed as if I were looking for snakes but I was really trying to make the distance to the stream seem shorter. The gravel was pink and out of the corners of my eyes I noticed how the trees were slipping past me and climbing out of the valley. To my right the cane had been cut and I squinted out at the mountains in the distance, feeling them move upwards into the sky. As I entered the valley, everything was leaving it. Behind me I felt the mountains and the cane whoosh up into the dome where everything was humming. They climbed higher, slowing gradually until they turned over themselves in a slow back somersault into the sea beyond the left side of the valley. The cane's whispering circled in the dome and down below the stalks seemed to be listening and nodding — as if they were discussing me and all the stalks were nodding in agreement. Whirring slowly in the heat, the sound descended in spirals from the dome and settled everywhere.

Suddenly I began to feel safe in the cane. I had lived with it all my life but there was something now that told me that it had spoken to me. I felt happy and it seemed happy to have spoken to me as if it had been waiting a long time to do so but hadn't had the chance. Now it was just us and we were friends. Perhaps it had made Mother late. It was as if the whole sky was humming.

This epiphany heralded a completely new sense of awareness. Somehow my resignation that I had been abandoned to walk home alone had triggered it off. The route was numbingly familiar yet I had always seen it from the perspective of a vehicle. My privilege had deprived me of any real contact. Now that I had to walk the distance, progressing step by step, the variety and complexity of my surroundings became apparent. Heightened by my initial feelings of vulnerability, everything demanded scrutiny. What had so often been dismissed as fields of boring sugar cane were now a multitude of growing stalks. Gradually, in the course of my journey, I became aware of objects beneath their natural superficial façades. Everything was magnified in both size and vividness and I established a microscopic view of the different metabolisms, all working, moving. In my childish way I sensed the osmotic diffusion in the cane cells; the slow flow in the phloem vessels; the undulatory swish of my cilia; and the steady coursing of corpuscles through the horses' veins as they snuffled at me from the neighbour's paddocks. Distant sheep were close. Sweat winked on a passer-by's skin and I felt the moisture. I joined the bees in the mimosa, hovering, holding. A sharp whinny of a horse followed me along the dusty road and I joined it, playing in the fine definition of my inner ears, filling my Eustachian tubes, releasing, regulating.

Although all this first appeared to me on that trip home from school when, for the first time, I was forced to make a major decision and control, albeit briefly, my destiny, much of it took years of gestation before I was equipped to assimilate its significance. Coddled by my upbringing, I had been oblivious of the environment that nurtured me until every-

44

thing was reduced by circumstances to essentials: a timid little white boy set on a four mile odyssey through fields of towering cane towards a haven which he had always taken for granted.

Like a fledgeling ejected from the nest, I was confronted by a new perspective. Hours of encapsulated trips amidst plastic-smelling upholstery and a console brimming with sweets while Mother tested me on my times-tables paled beside my slow vista from the dirt road of the endless fields of cane, the ominous gantry as it loomed over the cane trucks, the neighbour's homestead and sweeping paddocks, the fleeting conversations with passing blacks and the distant glare of our house's roof as it neared from across the hills. As everything became more familiar, so my appreciation of it lessened. Whereas the sheds and out-buildings on that occasion were virtually invisible, the no man's land between home and school remains indelibly branded in my memory.

Nowadays I must still check myself repeatedly; even familiar sights must always be looked at as if for the first time. Without these checks a person tends to drift, something which in our present circumstances could prove fatal.

Following instructions, I turn right onto a dirt road that winds interminably through rolling foothills splattered with huts. Scrutiny reveals a conspicuous lack of adult men. Like all reserves, this one is a catchment area for the urban industries. Women, children and the aged eke out a living bolstered occasionally by registered letters from their menfolk in the white sector. The hub has shifted; life here apparently continues at the first remove. But customs die hard and only the ignorant deny that these kraals retain importance. They are the heart of the matter.

Under the Land Rover's seat, in an oilskin beside the jack, I have hidden my revolver (the same one carried by Father during his arbitrations). Feeling the dashboard shelf to be too exposed, I have stashed the .32 away rather than use a shoulder holster. Moses has assured me that I'll be safe but I have taken the half precaution. Somehow, taking it on my person is too brazen. The last leg of my journey has been left open to fate. Perhaps just as well, because one never knows

45

what the sangoma will detect. What's to say that she doesn't already know. Perhaps she is radaring at this very moment.

Eventually I reach the meeting place, a trading store on a knoll above the Tugela. A crowd of blacks studies me quizzically; somewhere among them is my guide, an umfaan who is apprenticed to the sangoma. I stop the Land Rover beneath a Joko Tea advertisement. The yard is a mire strewn with beer cartons. An overladen bus detaches itself from a rank of clamouring vendors and groans past, slewing in the mud. Two maidens with breasts like cistern floats emerge from the store and, seeing me, giggle behind their hands. Suddenly, as if by magic, the umfaan appears.

'You have come from the sangoma?' I ask. He nods.

We set off along a succession of paths which ricochet through the landscape — skirting kraals, slicing fields and sliding through thorny thickets — until, after what seems like hours, we emerge on the lip of a cliff. Far below, beyond an orange blaze of aloes, snakes the swollen river, its ferocity dulled by distance. The umfaan glances back at me and then begins to scurry over the rocks like a dassie. I speed up, slipping between boulders whose positioning appears to be random. Would, I wonder fleetingly, an aerial view prove otherwise?

Suddenly a cave mouth looms. Dark and oval, it is thrown into stark relief by its pastel surrounds. There is an acrid stench of bat droppings and I shallow my breathing. The umfaan signals for me to wait and vanishes into the darkness. I watch his ragged white shirt bob down the throat. A ripple of bat squeaking shadows his progress. Two gnarled figs cling precariously to the cliff face and through them I catch shimmering glimpses of the river.

Presently the squeaking becomes hysterical. I adopt the military at-ease stance as I often do when I am self-conscious or nervous (in the caning queue at school, with strangers at a cocktail party). Perhaps the rigidity of the posture is supportive. What initially appears to be an animal emerges as the umfaan pushing a wheelbarrow containing a tiny, wrinkled marmoset woman in a hessian skirt and grubby bodice incongruously patterned with men and women riding penny-farthings. A fringe of charmed ringlets dangles down her puckered face. I avert my gaze briefly; then, resolving to stand my ground no matter what, I look her in the face. Her stare is withering. I avert again, focusing on her ruff of beads and inflated gall bladders. This is something right out of Rider Haggard. I stifle a nervous laugh, holding my breath as the umfaan lowers the barrow and asks in Zulu: 'You have the drink and the money?'

I hand over an envelope and the parcel. Two milky eyes record my every movement. An arm shoots out, seizes one of the bottles, and upends it among the wrinkles. She begins to wheeze and I watch the level drop alarmingly.

The sun breaks through the bank of cloud, giving the wet foliage a plastic sheen. I squint past the sangoma and into the cave.

The umfaan, like an actor in some epic drama, begins: 'Mother, this man has come to ask who it is that has been burning his cane.'

There is a silence followed by a long flurry of squeaking which, as it fades, transforms into a rapid high-pitched babbling. It is Zulu being spoken from deep in the throat of the cave. I make out the words 'I see, I see, I see' repeated at great speed until the resonance and echoes reduce them to a cacophany. The babbling begins to fluctuate between bass and treble and the words suddenly become 'a man, a man, a man' in rippling repetition. Another bout of bat squeaking intervenes and then fades. Presently the voice again emerges and 'who is to you what his forebears were to yours' is repeated twitteringly until the bats resume. I feel a tinge of goose pimples.

'Come closer,' demands the umfaan.

I edge towards the wheelbarrow as two tiny hands emerge from the hessian. Clasped in one is a cigarette with a match-head embedded halfway down its length. With surprisingly deft movements the sangoma lights the cigarette; the smouldering tip retreats slowly towards the match-head which bursts and flares when it is reached. The burning stump is tossed onto the ground.

'That is how your cane is set alight,' states the umfaan in

47

a matter-of-fact voice. 'The people are far away when the cane starts burning.'

The sangoma heaves and wheezes and retracts into the hessian. Silence follows. The murmur of the river can be heard beyond the occasional squeaks of the bats. The umfaan trundles the barrow into the darkness.

The sun has dried a crust on the dirt road and the Land Rover cracks it and allows the inner ooze to escape. I negotiate the fierce cambers, passing thatched huts, irregular fields of mealies and sweet potatoes, emaciated yapping mongrels and indignant chickens, from time to time having to change into low-ratio when the wheels sink and begin spinning.

A man who is to me what his forebears were to mine. Like a prep school mathematics riddle. It never occurred to me that the sangoma's answer would be so abstruse. Other planters had got more for their money: a man with a red shirt who will be visiting in your compound when you get home; a woman with a bad eye who lives with your induna. Mine is comparative; a man whose relationship with me resembles the relationship one of his forebears had with one of mine. There being no mention of intimacy, the culprit could merely be a chance acquaintance. A single meeting perhaps. I cast my mind back over the years, applying the divination's criteria. Remembering that appearances can be deceptive, I bundle friends and enemies together, treating them all as suspects. Finding several probables, I apply the forebear test which immediately acquits them. A blank. And yet how am I to know that the sangoma is correct? Perhaps she sees me as an exploiter of her people and has purposely misguided me. The spirits are notoriously fickle; perhaps they are having her on. Yet another possibility is that she is framing someone although it is unlikely. The whole venture has been a disappointment. I had hoped for something definite — a name, an obvious physical characteristic or speech defect, an exact whereabouts — like the other planters got, but this outcome remains as airy-fairy as most spiritual matters.

7

On reaching the tarmac, I turn left, gunning the Land Rover up a steep incline at the crest of which is a magnificent panoramic view of the Tugela several miles below the sangoma's eyrie and beyond it the rolling foothills of KwaZulu. Once the boundary between Zululand and the crown colony of Natal, the Tugela first had its importance diminished after the Zulus' subjugation in 1879 and then virtually cancelled with the implementation of the present government's homeland policy. KwaZulu has become an amorphous body of cells scattered throughout Natal, and the Tugela, a mere fraction of its former volume, just another river.

Among the kranzes below remains, I am told, a small population of leopards. Nocturnal and fiercely shy, they manage somehow to survive among the kraals, culling the monkey and baboon populations and snatching the occasional wayward goat. Perhaps among their number are several whose ancestors roamed what are now cane fields. Perhaps some of them would now be culling the monkeys at home had they not been evicted. Perhaps it would have been better had the whites never arrived, choosing instead merely to ply to and from the East, establishing at the most several coastal refreshment stations. Had the hinterland not beckoned with tales of inestimable wealth, perhaps the balance would, to a degree, have been maintained.

But the white man came, saw, conquered and stayed, leaving his descendants as natives of his adopted land. Only a privileged minority among us ever sees Europe and, faced with a cowed landscape, realises that it no longer belongs there. For the majority, Africa is the only reality. Some vacillate, living inconsequential lives in a restless limbo. Some leave for Europe seeking their own kind, only to return to this landscape and its peoples. The differences are huge: balmy English evenings have nothing on our hot effervescence of crickets and mosquitoes and the omni-present chance of a snake in the grass. An expatriate back in Europe longs for the cadence of a black's voice. But once home the politics stifle and the dilemma worsens. Caught between warring poles, the 'liberal' lugs about his conscience, suffering the disdain of his own race and the suspicion of others. But then national service intrudes, demanding a martial commitment. Like Michael I decided to do my stint rather than serve a prison term or leave the country. But un-like him I survived.

A man who is to me what his forebears were to mine — the possibilities are endless.

The road winds down through banana and sisal plantations. A sign announces Tamela and I can see the village in the valley. Once a stopover on the journey inland, it is now by-passed by the tar. At the height of the camber, I get an aerial glimpse of the squabble of roofs: a trading store, postal agency, magistrate's court, police station sporting its orange, white and blue tricolour, and a few 'railway' cottages. The recent allocation of the district to KwaZulu has stopped any development. White traders are compelled to sell out to blacks. Only the police remain and the magistrate pays occasional visits. Everything is frozen in transition.

Beyond the village, on a gentle slope dotted with thorn trees, is the remains of Fort Cockayne, one of the network of forts built during the Anglo-Zulu War. A square redoubt with two bastions at opposite corners, it had (according to Mad-bolt and Shannon) a clear, all-round field of fire of several hundred yards. Squatter shanties on the periphery of the village have transformed its south side into a defensive nightmare but a little imagination can obscure them. All that is still visible of the revetments are gentle, grassy mounds; a tree-fern still pin-points the nearby spring which was used then for water.

Since my meetings with Sarah began, this site has taken on an added significance. No longer merely of historical interest, it has become a spot which once, albeit briefly, accommodated her Harry. During my research, I located Harry's diary which contained the following entries:

50

Fort Pearson, Tugela, 4 January 1879
Major Martin has just spoken to me. I am to leave tomorrow morning to join my regiment at Helpmekaar. I am to travel south to Herwen and then inland past Manning's Post to Fort Cockayne which will be my first night's stop. I have the afternoon to organise things. The pont is at this moment nearing the far bank and I can see the men at Fort Tenedos loading things into wagons. It is devilishly hot. We killed two snakes in camp this morning, apparently mambas. I must write to Sarah.

Fort Cockayne, nr. Tamela, 5 January 1879
I left before dawn, riding alone. After collecting a letter from Captain Lucas at the Herwen hospital, I pressed on, reaching here late in the afternoon. It is now dusk. The scenery is magnificent. The rolling hills stretch away endlessly into the distance. About an hour ago I could make out the sea but the light isn't good enough any more. The fort is garrisoned by the Buffalo Border Guard, a rough bunch of locals. Their lieutenant, a huge bearded fellow whose parents farm near the Rorke's Drift mission, estimates that I should reach the General's column the day after tomorrow if I leave before dawn. We are, so I am told, having bushbuck for supper. It was shot this afternoon and I saw the cook skinning it shortly after my arrival. It has a chocolate coloured coat with white patches and short spiral horns. About the same size as an axis. One of the pickets is filling its water bottles at a spring down the hillside. Am longing for Sarah. I must write tonight and see if I can get the letter posted at Greytown.

Note the almost epistolary style of his diary. It is as if he is addressing Sarah as much as himself.

And so Lieutenant Harold Colville spent a night among those mounds a century ago while his wife Sarah continued her vigil far away in the Knuckles Hills. And so I, James Colville, head homewards where, fate-willing, Andrea will be waiting.

What image, I wonder, enabled the sangoma to answer my riddle? Did the culprit appear when the hag asked herself the question: 'Who burnt this white man's cane?' Was the man shadowed by his forebear? Did the sangoma conjure the solution in my presence or did she witness the crime 'live' as it were in her mind's eye and merely tell me the solution to my face to substantiate it? Did she know my problem — and its solution — before Moses had the message passed on to her? Thoughts whirl through my mind as my scepticism grows. A man who is to me what his forebears were to mine. It sounds ridiculous and yet, like Oedipus, I must solve the riddle.

8

Surely among a rich man's flowering lawns,
Amid the rustle of his planted hills,
Life overflows without ambitious pains;
And rains down life until the basin spills,
And mounts more dizzy high the more it rains
As though to choose whatever shape it wills
And never stoop to a mechanical
Or servile shape, at others' beck and call.

W.B. Yeats. Ancestral Houses

There must also have been a deluge inland. Far to the north I can see the brown smudge where the Tugela is disgorging itself into the sea. There will be sharks there. Spiralling in the murkiness, they will be butting and tearing the bloated carcasses. A sharks' banquet.

It is dusk. Andrea lies back, blonde and sleek-otterish in a wicker chair, her shoes kicked carelessly aside and her blouse unbuttoned. I lean back in my usual khakis, enjoying the sudden re-emergence of the night sounds in the lull in our conversation. Bats flick through the palms and bananas.

'Another?' I raise the J&B bottle and turn towards her.

She nods.

The vacant clinking of ice and crystal. The bottle spouts, spilling its contents down the sides of the tot measure, bursting onto the ice cubes in the two tumblers. The siphon rasps and the effervescent soda explodes onto the rotating swirls of prismatic light. The ice achieves weightlessness and surfaces. Bubble spires stream upwards, peppering air.

With a pale delicate hand Andrea lifts her clouded crystal to her lips, hesitates like a conjuror, and then with a controlled flick swallows half its contents. In a sudden surge of movement, she lights another cigarette and crosses and uncrosses her legs. For me it is an involuntary arc from coaster to mouth: a ceaseless inverted flesh-pendulum.

Andrea burps softly and giggles. I laugh and mockingly admonish her as she begins to tell me of her week. I sit listening in the gathering darkness, occasionally fading her out when the night asserts itself. Her voice, unlike Sarah's smooth sluicing, is a spirited torrent. Each day, she tripples, was mayhem, with one assignment after another. This morning's was a three-hour session for *Panache,* the new Johannesburg glossy. She, photographer Eddie, and two assistants drove out to an isolated mine dump on which a hired helicopter had been adroitly positioned. Changing in the back of the kombi into everything from undies and tangas to furs and gowns, she draped herself across the controls while prancing Eddie clicked. Then, back into town for a yogi-sip and out to the airport.

Like someone taking the waters, I let her rambling flow over me, being rejuvenated by its vigour. She pauses, nibbles several peanuts, pats Brutus who is curled up next to her, and sips her drink. Gratitude wells up in me; I am about to thank her for coming when I restrain myself. With the boat drifting smoothly, anything may rock it. Instead I focus on the darkness, imbibing the night. Flashing images of magnified cane stalks; blades of grass as large as banana leaves; crickets like terriers; vast neon clusters of fireflies and countless other vivid magnifications zoom in at me. The palms ruffle and the cane shuffles its stalks at the foot of the lawn, forming a sighing boma around the monkey chatter in the gully. Primitive rhythms throb up from the village among the umdonis, a wild joyous exultation of sound. Through half-closed eyes I watch the moths spiralling madly around the garden lights. The tink-tink of a fruit bat. Andrea looks at me quizzically and I mouth the word — bat. She nods. Briefly, light from through a shutter flares a gold stud in her earlobe. I listen for a bushbuck but Andrea intrudes with a hardy perennial:

'When are you coming to Johannesburg?'

'I can't during the cutting season.'

53

'But your indunas could keep everything going.'

'For a few days.'

'Then you could fly up quickly.'

'Perhaps in the off season.'

Season. The word hangs in the ensuing silence, then dissipates. I light a cheroot and stare abstractedly at Andrea. She is peering into the darkness, presenting an oblique view of her exquisitely structured face. Symmetrical to the point of measurement, each feature has a frightening fragility. As one would expect of a *haute couture* model, she is tall and elegant, not unlike Sarah but without the latter's intensity. Instead, Andrea has a sparkle which makes her visits so necessary for me in this time of decay. Despite this, however, our relationship merely plods on: she comes down regularly while I continue with my feeble excuses not to leave the farm. With arson rampant, no one here goes on holiday any more but I conceal from her the urgency of the situation, afraid of scaring her away with the truth. I need her visits more than I am prepared to admit. They are one of my few real contacts with the outside. She has strings of suitors on the Reef yet inexplicably she keeps returning. Perhaps I appear different, something of a recluse. Mystery intrigues but there must be more to it.

'Listen.' I pick up my flute and begin playing, my fingers moving weightlessly along it. 'Watch those eyes.' I point at the twin glowings in the flatcrown.

She watches them descend. The dance begins: the steps and shuffles in time with my music. And then it is gone.

Sarah will never appear when I am not alone. It is the first time that I have shown Andrea the dance and I turn to see her reaction. She is wide-eyed; that stage which preludes effusiveness. She alone — apart, of course, from Sarah — has shared this ritual with me. We have breached another block to our intimacy. Another step has just been taken despite its eventual futility.

The gong gongs in the hall and we go through for supper.

Moses, immaculate as always in his white uniform, pours the riesling and serves the lamb chops and vegetables. His attitude to Andrea has undergone a subtle change — no longer

54

is she treated as a guest but is now accorded a different, more deferential, status similar to that of the mistress of the house. Despite her only fleeting visits, she has suddenly risen in his estimation. Perhaps he has sensed my insecurity and is encouraging my relationship with Andrea in the hope that it will have the necessary stabilising and reassuring effect. I am heartened. Had Moses disapproved, or grown to dislike Andrea, everything would have been further complicated.

Andrea, still peaking on the bushbaby's dance, is brimming with questions: How did it start? Who trained the animal? The answer, I tell her, is simple. I merely, as part of my evening routine, took to playing the flute on the veranda shortly after dusk. It was soothing and I attempted to match my choice of music with the tempo of the night. One evening I became aware of an animal in the big flatcrown. It was there the following evening and then the next. As I finished playing it disappeared. Gradually I realised that it was actually attending my recitals. Becoming bolder it began to descend through the branches until one evening about a year ago it scampered onto the lawn, and, unprompted, performed its dance. Even when my recitals became irregular, I knew that every evening after dusk the bushbaby would be waiting in the flatcrown. I merely had to begin playing and it would descend and dance.

'But why didn't you show me it before?' she demands.

I shrug, noticing that she is moved by her inclusion, albeit delayed.

'Have other people seen it?'

'No.' A half truth. 'But you mustn't repeat it to anyone. It's a private thing between the two of us.'

'Alright,' she promises.

I can't help feeling guilty because I myself have violated a greater privacy. Somehow the dance had come to herald Sarah's visits, a sacredness into which I have allowed Andrea to intrude. But Sarah, of course, will remain distant this evening. Her presence will remain obscure.

Why I have shown Andrea the dance is, I suppose, because I want her gratitude. Although she is unaware of the sangoma's inconclusive revelation, it has depressed me and I need a greater intimacy than usual as a solace.

We retire early. Following the usual routine, she ruffles her bed in the spare room and slips naked across the passage to my bed, snapping off the bedside light as I toss my clothes over the shoulder of a dumb valet. Sitting at the foot of the bed, I finish my cheroot, knowing that she relishes the combined aromas of smoke and gun oil, setting the mood. She inhales deeply, dramatically. Now moonlight slices through the shutters, flaring the gold studs in her earlobes. I bite one gently. She swivels, leans forward and presses me with the taut softness of her lips. Her sudden movement causes her small breasts to swing forward. I begin fondling them in silence.

'What are you thinking about?' she asks suddenly, tilting her head to one side like a listening dog.

'Nothing really,' I reply for convenience.

'Stop it,' she demands. 'This is all that matters.' She holds my nose between her thumb and forefinger, playfully tugging it from side to side. Echoes of the neighbours — forget the future and all that.

'This,' she reiterates, squeezing my nose, 'this is now.'

'And so is this,' I add laughingly, kneading her breasts vigorously.

Tentatively I enter, pushing myself gently between. Entwined, taking opposites, we fluctuate rhythmically in our compromise. Lightness. Darkness. Lightness. We dapple with increasing intensity as I force myself to take stock of things. Here I am in Andrea, the person whom I hold dearest. I possess her while she possesses me. Like the scribbling inside my prep school Latin primer: this belongs to James Colville, Rangoon Estate, Manning's Post, via Nonoti, Natal, South Africa, Africa, Southern Hemisphere, World, Universe. It is she who is accommodating my itching ache as we move together. Her breathing shortens. Her mouth opens. Fillings glint, varnished with saliva. Her skin seems softer. I can smell her smell. She throws back her head. The slice of moonlight yet again catches the stud in her earlobe. The gold flares. We are alone in this shuttered room. Two creatures, we are copulating. There is nothing metaphysical about it;

like two ships we are moored alongside each other for mutual replenishment. She is feminine. I am masculine. Her receptacle receives my member. Our gentle friction mounts until the opposites blur blissfully and then slowly recede. We lie together, filmed in moisture which a breath from the shutter chills.

9

Saturday noon. The bell suspended from the myrtle near the workshop clangs. I stand on my office steps and watch the rapid evacuation.

Overalled figures converge on the drive — the mechanic and his assistants, gardeners, stable hands, the postman cum lawn mower, Rose the housemaid — and straggle down the avenue towards the compound and houses in the valley. A warm dreaminess envelops the suddenly silent yard. Bees are audible in the gums. Cattle low. Bantams sprout from the hibiscus hedge and begin scuffing the ribbed and zigzagged patterned footprints. A dusty flurry: a rooster mounts a reluctant hen, teeter-flapping and tail-shuttling, then struts cockily through a smudge of sump-oil, dissolving in the deep shadow of the grader.

I have given Moses the weekend off; Andrea enjoys her role as stand-in cook (it's fun cooking for two and all that). And it gives us privacy.

A black-shouldered kite circles high above the house. Brutus, like an aged wino, lies spreadeagled on the veranda. Through the open sliding doors I spy Andrea — longness in a candy-striped deck chair, a bangled wrist cradling a glass of riesling which refracts a glaring puddle onto the buffalo grass, no doubt prying into some tiny lives.

'It's swimtime,' she announces. A wayward strand of her hair, having escaped its clip, points earwards.

Sunlight sears the water's surface. I split the sheen and spiral in the thick coolness, seeing Andrea high above like an image in a vast melting stained glass window. Ripples of colour mirror my movements until I am half-lying on the steps, addressing her through a fringe of rivulets: 'Would you like to visit Isandlwana?'

'I sand wana. Do I wanna?' Tinkles of laughter.

58

'You know, it's that battlefield in Zululand where the Zulus gave the British a thrashing.'

'I donno if I wanna. Why?' Her American accent is appalling.

'I was thinking of going up in a fortnight. I visited it once years ago with my parents. I've been reading about it again recently and would like to see it once more. My great-great uncle was killed there.'

'Maybe.'

'May I, dear tippling madam, have the pleasure of a tumble with you among the cairns? We could take a hamper and get there by lunchtime; then go on to the hotel at Ulundi where we could have the dirtiest of nights. How does that grab you?'

'Intimately, but there is one proviso.'

'What?'

'That you eat your lunch today naked.'

'Done.'

She tugs off her costume, peeling off her panties in that feline, exclusively female way that is so straightforward and yet indescribable. I follow her buttocks and the zipper of her spine between the sliding doors. She has arranged the cold buffet on the sideboard: guinea fowl, wedges of pork pie, cheeses, salami, and an array of fruit and vegetables. Nibbling while Rome burns?

Two forms armed with plates, one fractionally tumescent despite restraint, move along the loaded sideboard, stacking food like lego players.

We settle in deck chairs (how I envy that magenta stripe its route behind and under her) screened from possible prying eyes by the retaining wall beyond the pool. Andrea is cheating; her sunglasses reflect my glances. Resembling Pearlstein models, we chew to the snick of cutlery, pausing frequently for slugs of riesling. At each swallow I trail each bolus past her epiglottis, down between her breasts to where it settles behind her navel. There the breakdown takes place. Little villi suck up nutrients that sustain her. All that is required is taken and the remainder snakes like a slow roller-coaster deep within her hips. Sometimes when, like a hunter listening at the ground for distant hoof beats, I press an ear to her stomach, I can hear the bubbling and squeaking inside as she decides on her requirements. To sustain her until Isandlwana.

High above the kite is still circling, watching our smallest movements. Perhaps it is Sarah or one of her acolytes sent to spy on the usurper. Perhaps she is that weightless speck skeining on the updraughts. As I think about her, I sense her everywhere: in the flatcrown, figs, flamboyants, magnolias and myrtles. She is annoyed. Our last rendezvous was long ago. She is missing her Harry. I am to blame for this breakdown. Whenever Andrea is here, I forget myself. But Sarah, our visit to Isandlwana is only weeks away.

What does the kite see? Probably two pink blobs in striped scoops on a greenness. Like one of those geometric riddles beloved of schoolboys: two concentric circles linked to another by a dotted line. The answer: a sombreroed-Mexican-pissing-into-a-tin. Ourselves in the same solution.

The afternoon is spent in the shuttered twilight of my bedroom. Two sweating bodies, and then sleep until tea at four. We wake torpid and glad of an opportunity of a walk.

We meander through the garden, under the pergola of jade vine — a favourite sunning spot of boomslangs at midday; they festoon themselves across the trellis-work, apparently asleep — to the paddocks where the Jerseys scrunch tufts of kikuyu or lie ruminating, chewing their cud-gum and listlessly flicking flies. Andrea never ceases to be amazed by their docility and, as always, comments on this, wagging a long manicured finger and exclaiming 'but they're so peaceful' as if they have no reason to be and her observation needs noting. Abstractedly she threads her fingers through my hair, patting me, no doubt transforming me fleetingly into a bovine companion, a mate with which she perhaps ruminates on that other world in Johannesburg, masticating the previous fortnight's happenings, hoping on the rebound to see them more clearly.

I catch my Europa's liquid ramblings in the surface tension of my pre-conscious, occasionally allowing little snatches to penetrate, replying while I scan the surrounding expanse of cane — the togt gang must weed there; that field needs cutting soon; there's some stunted growth, I must take a soil sample; those stalks are heavy, many have fallen. With our arms linked we wander along the contoured road with the bush below us. Towards the centre of the web of tree-tops is a shuddering movement. The monkeys are also back in this gully. More culling is necessary to check their insiduous advance.

Three black men pass. One of them greets us with a snarling accusative 'Ja' and I don't reply. When they are out of ear-shot, Andrea chides me:

'Why didn't you return that man's greeting?'

'Because he was rude. All he said was "yes", in a rather unpleasant way.'

'Do you know him?'

'No. He's probably a stranger passing through or visiting one of our chaps.'

'But why should he be rude to you?'

'Probably because he doesn't like me or what I stand for. His dislike can't be personal because I don't know him from Adam. He probably just dislikes whites. We are the oppressors. Even if he knew what party we voted for, it wouldn't make any difference. It's being white that matters.' I check myself suddenly; the explanation had gushed from me; the response perhaps of someone with a conscience.

'Weird.' Andrea has an endearing way of dispelling nagging, irreconcilable frictions with a casual label.

The blatant antipathy is relatively new. While there is no reason for that man to respect us, there is likewise none for him to be insulting. We are merely fellow travellers passing on a road. Although technically he is trespassing on my land — an ownership that he will most likely dispute — he is entitled to visit. So why the rudeness? Unlike many planters I go to considerable trouble to maintain good public relations, treating everyone with respect. Perhaps that is my fault: I have been born into a position of privilege but I am too insipid to remain successfully aloof. Would I be more re-spected if I were more dictatorial? Is kindness to the black labourer, as some planters feel, a sign of weakness? I am not a racist and yet I am the butt of racism. I am a loser in a posi-tion of privilege, hardly someone worthy of respect. Moses understands because he is mission educated but in the harsher reality it is survival of the fittest. This is my lair and I am defiling it through weakness — the sign of an animal doomed to extinction.

That the times are rapidly changing is something that I try and keep from Andrea. Let her continue to think of it merely as weird. It is so easy for her to dispel doubt that there is no need to foster it. Besides, she looks upon me and the farm as a refuge to which she can escape. Out of the frying pan into the fire, perhaps, but I am, as I have mentioned, anxious to maintain her dependence. Her presence is a balm. When she is here, I feel confident of peace beyond the deluge. When alone, nagging doubts sneak in, causing me to consider other, more negative, alternatives. What the hell? But then she is back and the burden lightens. Relief wells up although I know the truth and that her encouragement is based on ignorance. But groundless encouragement is preferable to prophecies of doom.

Later, on the veranda, Andrea pleads for an encore but the bushbaby doesn't appear — proof, I know, of Sarah's pique. Two's company. . . and all that. The table setting is the same: the J&B bottle, siphon, ice bucket, crystal tumblers, bowls of peanuts and biltong slivers. Brutus, having leopard-crawled under the table, waits expectantly for tosses of rejected gristle. Bats dart overhead, like flying-fish, on the surge of cricket song; fires flicker in KwaZulu and from the valley rainbows the glow of the sugar mill. There is, for some reason, no shift-change siren tonight, no linkage in the darkness.

On my study wall is an ink drawing of Isandlwana. Andrea reads the brass plaque tacked to the frame and uses her Yankee patter in an attempt to pronounce the name. I intervene, dissecting it, mouthing each syllable, curling my tongue against the roof of my mouth. She eventually masters the Zulu and with childish enthusiasm utters the refrain as I babble on about the battle. My recent reading at Sarah's prompting has rekindled my lifelong interest, making the war an obsession. Like an automaton I begin my exposition:

'It's strange how much the battle meant. So much that happened alludes to bigger things. The British Army was supremely confident and never dreamed that it could be beaten by a pack of savages. It was decimated. Only a handful of whites escaped. One regiment, Harry's, lost three times more officers than the most heavily hit regiment in all the Waterloo battles combined. Never before or since has an army with firearms been so severely beaten by one with primitive weapons. There was something of the tortoise and the hare about it because, despite their early victory, the Zulus were finished. They had humiliated the British who were more determined than ever to crush them, which they did at Ulundi. That's where we will be spending the night. So even disregarding Rorke's Drift and the death of the Prince Imperial, there is a lot to be learned from the war. In it the pendulum swung both ways and now the pendulum is at the end of its arc and poised to begin again. Tortoise and hare keep overtaking each other so that it's difficult to see which is which.'

I stop my babble. It is as though I have been speaking in tongues. Not really listening but buoyed up by my enthusiasm, Andrea demands a book on the war, wanting to do her homework in the fortnight before our expedition. As there is a party at the Umsundu Country Club next Saturday night, I have asked her to come down. She will, she explains laughingly, be available for lessons then. We kiss, mingling our whisky breaths as I edge her to the leather chair in the corner. Behind her is the drawing of the battlefield. The sphinx-like shape of Isandlwana hill rears out of the blonde wildness of her hair. She collapses backwards into the chair. On my knees I move to her while she supports the disaster on her shoulders.

Andrea left at dawn. Krish, the mechanic, is driving her to Durban airport from where she will fly back to Johannesburg. With the bed still smelling of her, I doze until Moses brings the tea at six. I have arranged for the sheets to be changed on Fridays so I can relish the presence (albeit fading) of her perfume for at least four nights. Strands of hair appear and are left undisturbed. As always, something that is taken for granted is missed when it is gone. We never learn. As with our surroundings, so much that exists now will soon become nostalgic memories.

Breakfast is once again a solitary affair. Bacon and eggs with a view of the pool through the sliding doors and beyond it the croquet lawn brindled with shade. The radio news rattles on but I phase it out; bombings and riots can manage without me until lunch. A gardener sweeps up the windfall of magnolia blooms, then scoops them into a sack. Like all of us, they are destined for the compost heap. On windy days the creamy heads form scurrying rafts on the pool. The tree is inordinately messy but felling it is inconceivable so both the gardener and I have become its servants.

I am in my office at nine. Seated at my desk, I confer with the indunas through the open window before moving to the dispensary. Eventually the queue is seen to, zinc ointment and gaudy laxative pills being the most commonly prescribed remedies. Anything serious is referred to the provincial hospital at Nonoti.

Then, my rounds of the sheds and stables. In the mechanic's absence, the two workshop assistants busy themselves with routine tidying. Stablehands sweep out the calf pens while a driver prepares the tractor-driven spray-race for the weekly dipping. Keeping the small herd has been uneconomical for some time but I maintain it for sentimental reasons. It is a vestige of that other more tranquil time when parents decided and I was left to perform my tricycle tricks for an audience of milkers. The surplus milk goes to the compound cook for distribution among the labour force. That in itself, I suppose, justifies its drain.

Next, my rounds of the fields. Brutus materialises and vaults from a tea-chest onto the back of the Land Rover. Taking the Holland & Holland with me in the cab, I head out along a series of dirt roads to the cutting. There's not a whiff of the monkeys. They are lying low, waiting for soft targets. They know well the value of hit-and-run.

On a steep hillside beyond the bush, the singing cutters are working their way into the cane from a contoured break. Advancing in extended order in a jagged rank, each repeats endlessly his felling/stacking routine: hacking several stalk bases, stripping each length of leaves with several practised slashes, then lugging them back across the trash to a stack which, on completion, will comprise his daily task. Later today or early tomorrow morning a tractor and self-loading trailer will winch on the stack and transport it to the mill.

Each cutter must contribute one load daily, getting bonus payment for all weight in excess of a prescribed requirement. Some of the more zealous among them, eager for double wages, have snapped axles with their contributions. With production of paramount importance, I cannot discourage them. Stronger axles are fitted as each breaks. Man versus metal.

With increased bonuses and the annual award of a bicycle to the best cutter as bait, there's no knowing the limit. I don't skimp on the bicycles either; they are among the best available. Consequently, I lose on the winner but win on the many runners-up. Note my disguised altruism. A charitable incentive brings home more bacon. That nkosaan gives away a smart bicycle each year, I can hear other planters' employees whispering enviously while I stash away the higher returns from the increased tonnages.

Leaving the Land Rover, I cross the trash to the induna for the daily record of absentees, and other sundries. Nothing is untoward, so our conversation is brief; then I move on to watch a crawler drag a tractor and trailer up the incline. The crawler's tracks jingle, the tractor accelerates in snorts, the taut cable crackles, and the cutters continue with their chanting. This euphony, laced with wafts of diesel fumes, is age-old and reassuringly normal.

Brutus shadows me back to the Land Rover. Lighting a cheroot, I drive off, taking a circuitous route along the boundary, past the previous Indian settlement, and back to the yard via the dam. A flotilla of yellow-billed duck glides through the lily pads and into the reeds. They continue nesting despite repeated raids by leguaans. Perhaps there is a lesson to be learnt from their admirable tenacity.

A fawn truck is parked in the yard. I know immediately that it's the police. Only their trucks have a grilled canopy, cow-catchers and protective screens. The driver's door opens and a familiar figure emerges — Sergeant Major van Deventer, the eyes and ears of the local station. Given to paying surprise visits to the farms in the district and listening over tea to the many anxieties, he knows as much as anybody about the tone of things. For how long has he felt the decline, I am tempted to ask but don't, knowing that years of drubbing have given him an impenetrability. Like all good policemen, his lips are sealed. Reputedly an anglophile, he has an almost Victorian courtliness which he probably reserves for the likes of me, it being taboo in the station.

'Mr Colville.' He strides towards me, a uniformed arm outstretched.

'Sa' major. What brings you to this isolated neck of the woods?' I ask, being purposefully purple, pandering to his passion for Englishness, playing the game.

'Just a routine check-up. To see how things are going out here on the farm.' His swaggerstick, clamped in his armpit, bobs as he speaks. As is customary, I invite him in for tea. We wander across to the house. Conversation thaws from awkward formality to natter.

'Any trouble?' he asks suddenly, getting to the pith. 'No problems with your labour?'

Moses enters with the tea. I pause, answering him only when we are alone again. Countering my previous decision to keep mum about the fire, I tell him all, including about my

66

visit to the sangoma. With the nonchalance of someone used to hearing convoluted confessions, he nibbles his rock-cake, inadvertently dropping a raisin into his tea. He doesn't interject, letting me ramble on, revealing much more than I intended to. After I stop, he lets the silence well up, sealing my statements. Then, with a 'May I?' he poises a hand above the rock-cakes. I nod and gesture expansively, and he takes another.

'You see, Mr Colville, times are changing and we must change our strategy to meet this new onslaught.' Appearing not to be in the least surprised by my revelation, including my visit to the sangoma, he takes a bite of his rock-cake and brushes the back of a hand against his moustache, further curling its horns.

'There is a very cleverly organised web of Communist terrorists who are infiltrating the sugar companies and farms and carrying out acts of sabotage and subversion. We know about them but every time we catch a few, more fill their places and the burning continues. It's just like a spider. We break a part of its web but the spider himself who sits in the middle repairs that section after we have gone. They sweet-talk the local blacks and get them to do the dirty work. Your fire was put in by someone in the district, maybe not one of your boys but someone from one of the next-door farms. If they got someone from outside to do it, he wouldn't have a good alibi if he were caught. You can't stop your labour visiting friends on other farms or stop others from visiting your compound. We can't arrest them for loitering or trespassing because they always have an excuse for being in a particular place.'

He is now in his stride but I halt him temporarily with an offer of a second cup. He nods — 'thanks'. I pour the tea as he rallies his thought-train and prepares to continue. His introduction has the glibness of indoctrination. There is obviously a general feeling of unease, despite the bombast of the other planters. He has been sent on his rounds to reassure us. Simultaneously, he has orders to prepare us for the worst without increasing our alarm. I pour myself another cup and settle back into the sofa, letting him run.

The cigarette method of starting a fire is old hat. It is now commonly used. The sangoma could have heard about it through the grapevine. He places little stead on her divination. I would be much better off now if I had reported everything to the police. They have informers. With all due respect, I was foolish to go to the sangoma. I was like someone with cancer who turned to black magic for a cure when I stood a far better chance with conventional medicine.

'Come to us, Mr Colville, you and we are all in the same boat.'

I agree, not through expediency, but because what he says is true. When the shit hits the fan, only colour will count. Where our sympathies lie won't warrant consideration. Perhaps I should be pragmatic and throw in my lot with the present system for all its faults. It may be racist and covertly anglophobe but it does have white survival as its cornerstone.

Support us through this troubled time. We need each other. Join the winning side. I have heard the rallying calls so often before and yet I must still reject them. I look the sergeant major in the eye and pledge my support. We have made a pact in which we are honour bound. He is pleased. Everything has been honourably concluded. We will keep in touch. I walk him back to his armadillo.

'Nothing is too small to report. Anything unusual, one of your boys behaving strangely, some stranger hanging around, get in touch. If there are any problems, you can always ask for me,' he says in parting and I thank him for his support. He leaves with a wheelspin and I watch him vanish into his own sirocco.

Krish returns at noon with news that Andrea's flight was delayed for an hour. He waited in the lounge until the aeroplane left and then headed for home. Even then, he seems to have taken an unnecessarily long time. I must check the Rover's mileage. Andrea will phone this evening; she will mention the delay then, if there was one.

I I

Thursday. Three days have passed since I last wrote anything. Writer's block has struck. Like all bogeys its timing is perfect. Knowing that adding to this chronicle has become a daily necessity, it darts in and thrusts home the dagger whenever I settle down at my desk. Consequently time crawls and the last three evenings have been a nightmare. I work myself into a panic during which only messrs Justerini and Brooks benefit. The enemy seems set on stopping me. After four tots I am ready to fight but at double that number my backbone crumbles. Only the knowledge that Andrea will be here again tomorrow keeps me going.

This morning after breakfast I tried again, keeping the indunas and the ailing waiting outside my office as I scribbled. As you can see from the preceding paragraph, the bogey magnanimously allowed me to acknowledge him. But with nothing else forthcoming, I decided to press on with my daily chores in the hope that sometime this evening I would be able to report the interim in the present tense, thus bringing everything back into line.

It is twelve hours later. The wind is high again, tremoring the dark fields and whistling through the shutters. Glows appear in the distance and the party-line is hot with use: after each ring-off comes a rush for the exchange. I am back at my desk, my fingers poised above the keys. Things are moving again. Today will shortly find itself on paper. My strategy has paid off. By bemoaning my fate, I have lulled the bogey; the mere mentioning of his name has gone to his head. His grip has slackened. Without his withering attention, my energies are welling up for the dam-burst. The recent past will soon become forever present, ably assisted by just enough J&B to ensure that the flow doesn't flag.

Thursday is ration day. With the non-tractor drivers also busy, I take the Land Rover into Nonoti to stock up with meat, tinned fish, bags of mealie meal, sugar (even sugar planters have to buy it), cabbages, flour, beans, etc. For as long as I can remember we have patronised Hamid Patel and Son, a burgeoning general dealer presided over by its patriarchal namesake, a splendid old gentleman beneath a red fez who always corners me in his labyrinth of sacks and packing cases for what he laughingly calls a 'business discussion'. He is a classic example of barrow boy makes good and his humble beginnings have left him with a clarity of vision so absent in many of us who have never known the other side. Pestered by scurrying bands of nephews, he takes me to his office — an elevated box poised like a guard tower above the vast shop floor — for tea and sticky buns.

Conversation covers everything: travel, investments, the waywardness of a particular relative who has called for his assistance, tax evasion and the loopholes in the currency control regulations, the cultivation of groundnuts, and inevitably, politics. He is alarmed by the gathering storm. He and I are on the same wavelength, so to speak, so he wants to hear my opinions. Where will I go when the going gets tough? When I am indecisive, he pesters me for a particular destination.

'I've actually thought of staying on and seeing it through. As in Rhodesia, things may straighten out after the transition. They have their problems but it must be a liveable place if one is prepared to change a bit.'

He guffaws and chides me for my innocence. 'You must be mad Mr Colville. Things here will become hell. Survival is all a matter of timing. If you get out at just the right time you can even gain on the move. But like me you are not sure where to go. And I was hoping to be enlightened.'

Between bites which leave his lips coated with vermicelli, he systematically dismisses all the possibilities: 'India — never; England — too old and cold; elsewhere in Africa — never; Mauritius — too unstable; Australia — perhaps, but they won't have us. You see Mr Colville, you and I are leftovers from colonial times, we are redundant, but unlike the others we have the blessing of vision so there is no excuse. I can discuss these things with you because you too are a man

70

of means with something to lose. I can't talk to my relatives and friends because they are either too stupid or don't think about the future. But we must think things over carefully and compare notes. Already it is too late but there is time if we make it. I have become soft. Years ago I would have been ten steps ahead.'

It is nearly noon when I pull myself away to the loaded Land Rover. Edging through the congested traffic of the Indian Quarter, I eventually reach the neat, avenued order of the white commercial district with its sedate bustle of shoppers and carefully monitored parking meters. Double-parking outside the bottlestore, I dash inside for a case of J&B and then head homewards.

The road from Nonoti into the hills rises slowly out of the mugginess of the town, switchbacking its way past deep old houses seething with wispish Indian children, mango trees with their glossy leaves, car and bus carcasses, and fluttering flags on tall bamboo poles. Slowly, reluctantly, the sprawling suburb succumbs to the ubiquitous cane. Labouring under its load, the Land Rover edges into the sighing greenness, rising and falling with its ebb and flow.

Clusters of palms indicate farmhouses hugged to their outbuildings by high hedges. Signs on the verge announce the company's sections — Carrickfergus, Quantock, Umsundu and Kerry Dale — each with its own manager, overseers, sirdars, indunas and army of labourers. Next the polo club, its team once provincial champions, holders of the Waterford Cup, but now fighting relegation to the third division. Then the company hospital with its two white doctors and shuttered wards, and the little St John's Church with its cemetery. Planter families lie neatly in rows while the Indians' crosses wander from the bottom fence into a grove of gums.

Gradually the air becomes more rarified. Coolness jets through the vents. Far below to the left the Umvoti River coils through another finger of KwaZulu which was a hotspot during the Bambata Rebellion. Now overpopulated, overgrazed and rutted, the valley looks idyllic to strangers crossing this neck miles above it. There is a lay-by from which tourists can take photographs of the picturesque hutted kraals. As

71

with anything gross, distance placates the onlooker.

After another steep ascent I reach Manning's Post, the local trading store and bus terminus where each morning one of the gardeners collects the newspaper, and returns in the afternoon for the post. The familiar sign — Rangoon Estate — is on the right, swaying gently from twin chains above the T-junction. Beyond it spreads a neighbour's plantation of bananas, the ripening bunches swathed in hessian.

The wide district road with its harsh all-weather surface bisects the farm and descends to the mill in the valley. Around it capillaries a network of private roads and cane-breaks. Continuing past the mouth of the avenue, I weave along a series of overgrown tracks to the cutting where I consult with the induna. Several men are absent; otherwise all seems to be well. A tractor and loaded trailer move slowly across the row corrugations and I dart ahead of them, doubling back to the avenue.

As I enter the vaulted shadow, a puff adder is crossing the pink gravel, writhing its chain pattern across the open ground. Hideously distended like a length of diseased bowel, it hurries as the Land Rover approaches, entering the path of the right front wheel. To continue would mean popping it, but I decide against it, bearing fractionally to the left as it disappears into the undergrowth bordering the Indians' houses. Why the sudden magnanimity? I ask myself, but the answer. isn't forthcoming.

The lunchtime bell clangs as I pull up outside the ration room. I light a cheroot and sit smoking in the cab as the rations are unloaded. The relieved springs bounce as each bag is lifted off. Why save the snake? I ask myself again as the answer appears like a spectre from the smokescreen. That a snake is a snake is no fault of its own. That I am what I am is no fault of my own. To be born a white on a black continent in a time of dissolution was not of my choosing. Conversely, to be born a black here during a period of increasing racial consciousness was none of the insurgents' choosing. They are what they are as I am what I am. We have our roles to play, as does the snake. I am impressed by my deduction. Everything is neatly slotted, assuming a transitory order before I

72

query my attempts to cull the monkeys. Then, like most theories, this one springs a leak.

Lunch is cottage pie. Moses, like the perfect compere, unobtrusively assures smooth continuity. Again I ignore the radio news, keeping its mumbling on the fringe, hearing the intonation but not the gist. Repeatedly I find myself musing over my two recent encounters, each so different and each offering its own reaction to a mutually acknowledged deterioration. Join the laager, urges Van Deventer while old man Patel advocates gapping it. Both opinions, I tell myself, have their merits, but I prefer the latter, admiring the old man's pragmatism and lucidity. Unlike the sergeant major, he isn't fuddled by a cause.

Needless to say, however, neither is altruistic in his intentions. Each needs the reassurance of my presence in his solution. Every convert bolsters. I am flattered but not fool enough to ignore the other reasons. Being a grey figure in this largely black-white confrontation, I need pulling into line. Hence Van Deventer's recent interest. Similarly, Patel's curiosity is aroused. My fence-sitting, he feels, must conceal some ingenious wrangling. My apparent indifference demands it. No liberal sits tight without something up his sleeve.

But ultimately I must please myself and decide whether to take the airlift or ride the storm. In one of my lucid moments now, I plump for the latter, prepared to chance the angry swell. For all its indecisiveness, it remains a decision and I am proud of it.

I 2

I am out here on the veranda with Sarah. A nightwatchman passes, circling the Club, plodding on like an ox operating a threshing device: the threshing inside, his crucial patrolling outside, eyes skinned for the tell-tale crackle and billow in the cane. A palm frond scrapes rhythmically against its bole like a metronome setting the night's pace while the music inside continues its parody endlessly. Sarah has forgiven me the setting, understanding my essential solitariness. I turn from the hilarity to a distant mumble of drums, relishing her proximity, imagining a lavendered silkiness at the nape of her neck. She withdraws, leopard-purring, and recedes into the darkness.

I don't need to go inside to know what they're doing. Their antics are as clear as daylight. Everyone's there, messrs and mesdames Herd, Baren, Dopping, Pace, Bevy, Muster, Nide, Kindle, Sounder, Covey, Down, Wisp, Pride, Cete, Sord, Clowder, Fall and Chattering, with assorted new couples, whose names I don't know, and a siege of singles. And Andrea.

As always there are several groups, each with its own kinetic energy and *raison d'être*. One comprises men only and hovers in the hall, poised between the bar and the main lounge where the women are divided neatly into two groups, each with its subtle pecking order. Character inter-relationships and the private planter/company employee juxtaposition largely determine the stratifications. Whereas the planters are inherently more wealthy, many of the top company officials enjoy a greater status; their resultant smugness is fanned by increasing insecurity as retirement age nears. Whereas the men have partly drowned their differences in a growing camaraderie — although the most talkative are invariably the seniors — the women just maintain their gossamer veneer. Side by side in the lounge, each group appears self-contained

74

while its members are surreptitiously weighing the other's participants against their own exclusion.

Year after year they repeat the pantomime to the accompaniment of the tripping tinkle of pianos and the sweeping zwinging of violins. Scoots of Indian waiters zigzag like marbles through the bagatelle board of grotesque exaggerations: a shrieking madam with huge tits sheathed in lamé and dripping with sequins; the bumbling director with his perennial theory on quotas, the fresh flash-flash of the mill manager's daughter recently returned from a no-name finishing school; and the syrupy swagger of yet another successful son back from Cirencester without a diploma. Up jumps Mrs Bevy with a yahoo for the conga and the slumberous snake uncoils itself and begins its shuffling meander through the tambotie tables and tired Morris chairs. Down, down drink the lads in their corner — the younger on the man's brand and the older pink with pinkers.

To the unpractised eye everything appears convivial. Everybody is having fun. These are members of a united community which will endure. Even the wiliest punter will favour its odds. But inexplicably only I seem to notice the cracks.

It is later and I am still on the veranda. Andrea is with me; she is peaking and full of talk of Willy's dancing. She downs her drink and rushes off for the next whirl. My not dancing has condoned her availability for partners. But, so I'm told, Willy is King. I find a J&B and climb into a hammock suspended between two of the veranda pillars. Why not go inside? you may well ask. And I ask it of myself all the time. What will they think? He comes along with his dolly-bird from Jo'burg and then sulks on the veranda while she has a whale of a time. My answer: I only came to do my bit, to show that I am still part of the community now that things are supposedly getting a bit rough. Although you wouldn't think it from the highjinks inside.

The sugar community is strange. All that remains of the magnificence of the sugar baron days is this jaded false opulence and yet, either oblivious of our uncertain future or perhaps motivated by it, everyone is roistering through the early decline into paralysis, determined to continue until the

75

inevitable dead stop. Nobody dares look at the causes of our predicament. Let's fiddle madly because Rome will burn anyway. Perhaps they are right. Perhaps I am the prophet of doom who is getting himself tied up in knots about the inevitable. My coming tonight was a mistake. In my attempt to appear one of the community (and show off Andrea), I have emphasised my incompatibility with it. Plainly and simply, I am an outsider, not through any romantic selection but merely because something inside me rebels at the futility of all this brouhaha. Perhaps the deficiency is mine. Perhaps there is no cause for alarm or perhaps, like Cassandra, the last laugh, if it can be called that, will be mine. Only you will know. Will you be nodding sagely at my acuteness or be scornful of my whimpers? Still, this J&B declares that everything's fun and to hell with the arsonists. As another gulp disappears inside me, I wonder where Andrea is as she appears suddenly around the corner as half of a swaying duo emulating the tango. She winks at me over Willy's shoulder as the dodgem collides with an urn and ricochets out of sight.

Just over a decade ago my friends and I had rocked late into the night out there on the pool veranda. Wet with sweat we had slipped into costumes and swum, after first using torches to check the water for snakes. The pool now has lights which animate the surrounding flatcrowns. Their installation is one of the few improvements. Otherwise there is a subtle decay. Obviously the contributions aren't what they used to be. The money is still here but what seems to have crept in is a greater reluctance to part with it. Perhaps the usual surplus is now being channeled overseas by those shady Kenyan agencies who claim forty percent. Perhaps it is being frittered away on luxuries in a last fling. As usual only time will tell. Of us here only you will know our motives.

Another, much earlier memory, also has this setting. Escaping from the Humber in my pyjamas, I crept timorously across the dark lawn as fairy lights (burning candles in brown paper bags) twinkled down the driveway. Shuffling up these stairs in my slippers, I wandered into the glare of the hall. Lovely ladies with nice smells and red lips all turned and looked. Waiters, dark in their white clothes, stopped. Mother's voice: 'James, if you're a good boy you can have the head of the meringue swan in the morning.' A chorus of goodnights. Back came the darkness as Father carried me across the lawn. When the car door closed, the music stopped.

Today's gravitation is in the opposite direction. Once a moth, I have undergone a metamorphosis and like a pupa now prefer darkness instead. It is well after midnight before I manage to extricate Andrea and escort her unsteadily away from the glare and into the palms. With sausage fingers I start the Rover. After stalling once, I edge it down the avenue and toot-toot. The headlights silk across the boles, eventually arcing into the cane. I hear them back there behind us going on about what a pleasant girl she is while he is such a strange chap. Surely they aren't compatible? sings the chorus. So much for my little intended ostentation. Andrea collapses across from the passenger seat, cupping her head in my lap and falling instantly asleep. On through the darkness. Despite my dozen J&Bs, I find myself unusually awake and vigilant for a log across the road. Several weeks ago a couple was assaulted through the use of that ploy. Luckily, another car arrived in the nick of time. Although the newspapers regarded it as merely another mugging, I feel otherwise as I'm sure do the police and others in the know. Only the likes of those at the Club demand that it was an isolated incident.

Dust, made strangely luminous by the tail-lights, tumbles in the rearview mirror. A stirring. I look down. Andrea smiles, mouthing words: 'Stop please darling, I'm popping.' I brake. She slides across and opens the passenger door. A gust of the night and its sounds. Scampering to the verge, she stops, drops her hands to her sides, draws up the skirt of her long maroon dress and, as she squats, slips down the band of her panties to her knees. From the snug interior I watch her pale flanks in the moonlight, imagining the soft sound of her gush and the even softer dab-dab of the lilac tissue. Riveted, I stare at her, yet it is more than voyeurism. With her quick exposed, I have become party to a deeper intimacy. It is as if I have surprised a duiker giving birth. Unable to escape, the animal continues, oblivious of the consequences, subordinating its instincts to trust. Andrea performs a solitary chore under my scrutiny

77

rather than behind the open door. As often before, we share the experience, but tonight's seems somehow momentous and enriched by its implications. Dropping my guard briefly, I am too involved to fear the chance arrival of an intruder. Suppose that a labourer surprises us. Should he come across the idling car and Andrea at her business while his employer watches, what, I wonder, would his reaction be? Despite the banality of the act, it could make him snigger: 'Look, there's the nkosaan's girl pissing. Look at that white woman pissing.' Stifled ribald laughter. Perhaps, under my gaze, he will bottle his mirth until back with his friends in the compound. Is my assessment of Andrea's vulnerability rational or warped by my environment? Am I unreasonable to assume that the black labourer will snigger? Perhaps, but there is something more: although mundane in the extreme, Andrea's act has been made momentous by our (the whites) projected purity. Had we gone native, it would be nothing. But like the indiscretions of a libidinous nun, our secrets are newsworthy. We have entangled ourselves in our web of supremacy. We too must dance to the tune we have called.

Andrea snuggles back and has again dropped off when we arrive home. The nightwatchman's torch flickers from the stables towards the workshop. Brutus snuffles out of the darkness, smearing my trousers with spittle in a hearty welcome. I lift Andrea and carry her along the veranda. Despite my unsteadiness, I manage to keep on the rails.

We are soon in bed. Andrea falls asleep immediately while I pick up Lady Gregory's *Journals* and read on, absorbing none of the entries but being soothed by the words. Through the shutters I can hear the faint voices of bushbabies, owls, nightjars, bushbuck and vervets. Down the passage, in the hall, the grandfather clock chimes an indiscernible number. There is a pervading smell of gun oil and a faint glow of moonlight reflects off Sarah's framed face, animating it although I know of necessity that she must be mute tonight.

I switch off the light. Andrea is warm beside me. Despite the repercussions, I have forgiven her her behaviour at the party. In a fit of magnanimity, I confess that I was the culprit; I made the stage on which she danced and am thus responsible for her evening with little Willy, last of the sugar barons. A millionaire several times over, he is a hardliner whose draconian labour policy is notorious throughout the district. Never one to spoil his cutters, he refuses to install even the most rudimentary facilities in his compounds, naively imposing the public school ethos in the name of discipline. Petty rules curtail their freedom further. I have spoken to him on several occasions but he swears by his methods. When the time comes, they can always cite the likes of Willy when pressed for a reason for their mayhem. Quite right, objective observers will admit, the whites had it coming to them. But what of us who try? is my plea. Must we too be drowned in the deluge? You know as well as I do that the answer is yes.

A man who is to me what his forebears. . .

13

A fly dithers along *Turbott Wolfe*'s spine. I watch it for a minute or so, then doodle; anything to avoid continuing with this chronicle. Despite my compulsion to crystallise this little world, it is becoming increasingly difficult. As with like poles of a magnet, the typewriter and I repel each other. Suddenly, in an unusually decisive move, the fly flits across to the Isandlwana painting and scuttles weightlessly over the carnage. I follow its faltering zigzagging and what appear to be brief pauses for preening. The gecko who lives on the cornice above the standard lamp — an old friend who has long watched my laboured attempts — takes the offensive. Stalking diagonally down the wall, it hurdles the frame, lashes the fly, and returns to its corner. Somewhere in the gully a bushbuck barks. I listen consciously and it barks again.

Of all the causes of the Anglo-Zulu War, says Daniel Harris in his *The Rattling Of The Shields*, fear was the most important. Determined to do my homework before our visit to the battlefields, I have read his definitive account from cover to cover during the last week. The Natal colonists, says Harris, lived in dread of an invasion by Zulu impis from north of the Tugela. Missionaries working among the Zulus told tales of the restoration of the legendary war machine and the brutality of its punitive raids. With the fear at fever pitch, war became inevitable. Bartle Frere, high commissioner for South Africa, picked the fight and got it.

Ponderously the British and colonial troops mobilised and began their three-pronged advance into Zululand: the left column from Northern Natal; the centre — including Lord Chelmsford and his staff — at Rorke's Drift; and the right column up the coast towards Eshowe. Each was to march on Ulundi, simultaneously giving lateral support to the others. A fourth column, consisting largely of native levies, was to remain at Middle Drift and await orders. The plan was

80

admirably simple: engage and defeat the enemy, then sack the royal kraal. In a matter of weeks it would all be over and peace assured.

It was to the right or coastal column that Lieutenant Harold Colville — Sarah's Harry — was seconded. Having boarded a troopship in Colombo, he arrived in Durban with only days to spare. What is known of the column's advance is taken largely from his meticulously entered and annotated diary which Harris acknowledges in his bibliography.

Appearances are deceptive: for all Harry's apparent conventionality, his diary is remarkably perceptive. The freshness of his observations gives them a profundity. Perhaps he wasn't such a twit; I concede a point.

Hampered by the numerous swollen rivers, the column lumbered up the coast with its wagon train trailing across the rolling hills. Establishing forts at various intervals to protect the supply route, it continued to Eshowe where it was soon to become beleaguered. Harry was left at Fort Pearson, an earthern redoubt on the south bank of the Tugela. With orders to assist in the bivouacking of troops as problems with the pontoon had created a bottleneck, he reluctantly settled down to a supportive role until his return to his regiment in the central column at Helpmekaar. Within days, he was at Isandlwana.

And so fate, with its usual guile, manoeuvred young Harry across half the globe to his death. Despite the infinite possibilities of escape, its conjuring ensured that his course kept true. Like an animal for the slaughter, he was transported to a distant abattoir where the price was highest. Sarah, like many bereaved loved ones, blames herself. Why she didn't prevent him from leaving has remained her millstone. That he wanted to go, she ignores. It was her fault. Had he merely slipped off the gangplank on embarkation and been crushed between the heaving ship and the quay, would she have blamed herself so vehemently? I doubt it. The savagery of his death demanded retribution. Newspapers told of the Zulus' disembowelment of their victims. One nightmare followed another. With the army being too amorphous for a scapegoat, she lapsed into self-hatred. Years of near silence and sombre clothing became her penance and her guilt ensured a restless soul. I have it to blame, or thank.

Andrea and I are planning our expedition meticulously like military logisticians. I have made several special trips into Nonoti for the ordinary grub while she combs Johannesburg delicatessens for exotic tasties. Every evening we liaise by telephone, hogging the party line and infuriating the neighbours.

I have also been poring over road maps of Natal and Kwa-Zulu, searching for the most economic route, wanting to cram as much as possible into our two days. The following tentative itinerary has been submitted to Andrea who giggled at the string of names and gave it her blessing: after an early start, we head via Tamela, Greytown and Tugela Ferry to the military cemetery at Helpmekaar. Then Rorke's Drift for morning tea, Isandlwana for lunch and Ulundi (via Babanango) by mid-afternoon, checking in at the hotel in time for a rest before dinner. On Sunday, after a leisurely start, a slow meander via Eshowe to Fort Pearson, then Nonoti and home. In all a circuit of about 560 kilometres.

Andrea will be arriving as usual on Friday afternoon. Moses will pack the Rover under her supervision. Then Andrea and I will have our customary sundowners on the veranda before supper and an early bed. New sheets await glossing with her perfume. Such is the run-down but like all campaigns there will be snags and the need for compromise.

Leaving the farm during these troubled times, albeit for only two days and a night, involves considerable organisation. Moses is entrusted with the house, Brutus and the garden; the indunas are responsible for the labourers both at work and in the compound; the chief stableman has the cattle as his charge. Everyone is in turn answerable to the mechanic who has the use of the Land Rover and has been instructed to contact a neighbour should an emergency, such as a fire, arise. Beyond that nothing much can be done as a locum is only worth employing for a period of at least a month.

At last it is dusk on Friday. Andrea is opposite me on the veranda, draped in a wicker chair, gently raking Brutus's back with her toes, each nail like a shear lifting and parting his brindles. The evening's sounds gather unobtrusively as we natter, tossing back J&Bs. Andrea sparkles, excitedly interspersing *haute couture* scandal with recently garnered facts about the Zulu campaign. Prancing Eddie's gay abandon finds its counterpoint in a snippet about Colonel Evelyn Wood, commander of the left column.

'Did you know that a giraffe once stepped on his face? It was in some zoo in India. He was trying to ride it as part of a bet. His cheek was slit open to the teeth and his nose was crushed.'

'No,' I answer, as she bubbles on about other peculiarities.

'His life was charmed. He was wounded countless times, caught every possible disease, and still lived on into his eighties.'

Who, I wonder, prescribed all his chances when Michael had only one? Are our lives as charmed? Now that the storm is really gathering, we will need all the luck we can get.

The gong gongs for supper. There is no mill siren again, I notice, as we move indoors. Just the night sounds and the darkness, both of which vanish as the door closes. In the sudden quiet of the hall, I pause, pecking Andrea lightly on the cheek, sniffing her deeply before we enter the dining room where Moses waits with news that the Rover is packed.

It is a guinea fowl night. Having had kedgeree last night, I know. Mellowed by our sundowners and several quick glasses of riesling, we both become more animated still. Briefly objective, I watch our effervescence, flippantly chiding Andrea for making me drink too much; tomorrow will be a long day. Laughter.

Before coffee in the sitting-room, I use the guest's powder-room (one of Mother's modifications; it used to be a pantry). Once again detached, I watch my jet of piss with slow puzzlement, drawing the taoist symbol of the Great Ultimate in the pan, frothing the water.

Back in the hall I find Andrea and Moses deep in discussion. With his family kraal not far from Isandlwana, he knows the area well. A number of his ancestors saw action in the massacre, at least one in a position of authority. Thanks to the Zulus' oral tradition he has many stories to tell. Andrea is enthralled. Do I know that I have an authority in the house?

'Of course,' I reply, 'and he is of patrician stock.'

'What?'

'Blue-blooded.'

We are in bed by ten. After a giggling romp we are soon asleep. Like children on Christmas Eve, we are expectant of tomorrow.

14

Rorke's Drift. In the small settlement under the Oskarberg are outlined the defences as they supposedly were during the battle. Parking the Rover in the shade of a thorn tree below the buildings, we wander up through the hallowed remnants, reading a trilingual plaque — English, Zulu, Afrikaans — lazily linking words, allowing the shimmering heat and electric insect sounds to penetrate the journey's residual fug. Black students from the art school meander along dusty tracks as a swarm of spreeus wings noisily overhead, arrowing for the drift itself.

Finding a small stone kraal enclosing an obelisk, we read the roll of honour, mouthing the Englishness of the names, repeating them, their ranks and regiments like a litany in the humming silence. Mulling over how much more effective these humble memorials are than their ostentatious Afrikaner counterparts at several sites nearby, I am about to mention this to Andrea when a sudden thudding causes me to look upwards: high on the crown of the Oskarberg a rock, having dislodged itself, slides and bounces down the gradient.

Andrea, having noticed the art school shop, scampers towards it with a bargain hunter's urgency, fearful of being pipped despite our being the only visitors. By the time I reach it, she is flapping through the piles of carpets, eyeing each colourful combination of geometric patterns with an eye to her Johannesburg flat.

'Would this,' she asks, holding up the corner of an ochre-sienna combination, plucking at my khaki shirt, 'go with my kelim and Khnopff's *Sphinx*?'

'Perfectly,' I answer abstractedly, my memory of her flat's décor misted by the intervening years. On shelves beyond the mats is an array of pots. Why her flat and not home? I ask myself, realising simultaneously that with a little effort the fusion could be made. The young attendant sucks a ball-point and watches us bemusedly.

A cry from the Oskarberg picket. Soon a rattling murmur loudens until it is deafening. The uThulwana, uDloko and iNdluyengwe round the mountain and, frenzied with blood-lust after their enforced passivity at Isandlwana, surge towards the barricade. Like waves of molasses, the youngbloods rush at the stacked mealie bags, being felled by the volleys and the frantic bayonets. Again and again come the rushes but the thin red line holds. At dusk, the redcoats retreat to the inner redoubt, abandoning the hospital building whose thatched roof the impi sets alight.

Andrea signs a cheque while the attendant rolls up the carpet, tying it neatly with string. With the transaction completed, I lug the purchase back to the car while Andrea bubbles excitedly beside me. Then tea. Placing a billy filled with water on an army burner (national service does have its perks), I sit back against the trunk of the thorn tree and let her take over. With one eye on her outlined haunches as she bends into the boot for something, I absorb the peacefulness: the warmth, insect buzzings, dust, and the distant music of voices. The tea in its enamel mug, like the finer fare on an evening out, seems that much better in these surroundings. Discussing the battle, we attempt to imagine things as they were that January afternoon when, after the Isandlwana massacre, a handful of troops repulsed the rampant impi, preventing an invasion of Natal.

'If you were here then, would you have stayed and fought or made a dash for it?' asks Andrea pointedly, but twinkling.

'The latter,' I reply with rare dogmatism, pointing into the distance towards Helpmekaar. 'You wouldn't have seen me for dust.'

'But what about your VC? You had a one-in-ten chance.'

'Aah,' we both utter, laughing, apeing the participants in a television commercial, 'aah.'

Gazing at the mission chapel, I find myself wondering whether my tent-mates and I would have offered such spirited

86

resistance had it ever been necessary during our stint on the border. Despite obvious necessity, those Victorian troops had a mission (albeit often only a career) which many of our conscripts seem now to lack. The confrontation is basically the same — white oppressor against black aggressor — but all except the hardcore right wingers and the usual proportion of bellicose youths now merely go through the motions.

Firing the hospital roof was a fatal mistake. Well into the night the flames illuminated the redcoats' field of fire. On and on with almost fanatic resolution the warriors rushed at the bagged redoubt only to be beaten back with heavy casualties. When the fire finally burnt itself out the impi burst up against the bags under cover of darkness but yet again the bullets and bayonets prevented a breach. After midnight the rushes slackened but desultory sniper fire from the Oskarberg kept the defenders pinned down until dawn when the impi retreated. Legend has it that the barrels of the defenders' Martini Henrys glowed through the night while on occasions rounds baked in the breeches, discharging before the triggers were squeezed. Mounds of Zulu dead ringed the defences. The honour of the decimated 24th had been regained.

Before leaving we decide to take photographs. With professional ease Andrea glides from prop to prop — lounging on a low stone wall, standing beside the plaque, caressing the obelisk — as I become an Eddie surrogate, catching her litheness below the Oskarberg, using perspective to lessen its looming. Then, at her insistence, I smile self-consciously for a single snap. Harry's absence from this battle demands this objective response; at Isandlwana we must experience everything firsthand.

Keeping to schedule, we are gone by noon. On either side of the gravel road stretch wide grasslands whose expansiveness is so different from the undulating patchwork-precision of cane fields. It is another peripheral area jigsawed with pieces of KwaZulu, far from the white belt of the central Natal midlands, and I notice that most of the names on the signboards beside entrance gates and cattle grids are Afrikaans. Although these farms — I remember Father saying — were predominantly owned by English-speakers during his youth, few of that hardy strain have remained, most of them having migrated to the cities or safer rural areas. Then back came the Afrikaners, accustomed to hardship and bolstered by a benign Land Bank and faith in their government.

At a T-junction I point out to Andrea a crumbling building and the foundation slabs of several others amidst erosion slashes and tussocks of dry grass. A black youth lies in the shade of a single gum sapling while his charge, a straggle of piebald goats, bleat and crop among the remains.

'On our last trip,' I begin, 'Father pointed out those ruins to us. They are apparently the remains of a flourishing home-stead-cum-trading business. The sons were at school with him. He once spent a holiday with them here. We stopped for a picnic and while Mother prepared things, Father took Michael and me on a guided tour, pointing out the tennis court and describing the rooms from the pattern of the foundations. He even found the position of the billiard table, pointing out the cement bases for its legs. There were two sons and a daughter. If I remember correctly, he said that the elder son, who was his classmate, ended up as a policeman in Sarawak and the younger joined the British Army and was later crucified by the Irgun in Israel; the daughter married and went to live in Durban. Apparently when the old man died and this area was handed over to KwaZulu, the mother also moved to Durban. I don't know why the buildings were demolished, but I think. . .'

'Let's go back. Take *me* on a guided tour,' interjects Andrea excitedly but it is late and I decline. We must keep to schedule.

On rounding a corner, I catch sight of Isandlwana hill in the distance. Rising like a sphinx from the low surroundings it seems a strangely apt choice of host for a heroic clash, as if its primordial formation was for that purpose alone. I point out the brooding silhouette to Andrea who burps and laughs.

15

All in the lee of Isandlwana hill, riveted by its blunt features, bateleurs swoop and lessers niggle from nests in its rocky flanks. Chicks swivel in their twiggy cups, dolloping white streaks towards the dassie chinks. From among the cairns, sienna dongas rip the grassland towards the groin. A herdboy meanders through the waving tips, tossing cries into the wideness towards Hlazakazi and Silutshana. From behind the sentinel comes the soft tolling of the St Vincent's Mission bell. All under the spell of a lesson well learnt a century ago. Everywhere the dignity of lives lost while aweful visitors beneath the looming sphinx talk deferentially of the spirit of the place.

Chants and rattles. Salvoes greet the thundering surge. Red squares sally forward, brace, hold, then withdraw to ledges against the haunches. Suddenly a solar eclipse. A hesitation in the brief twilight, then again the splatter and roar. Black pincers open, encircling the sphinx as red figures run for the river. Among them Lieutenant Colville, hugging a bay gelding, galloping through the stabbing, slashing from its withers at the uDududu who are ever eager to wash their spears.

Our open wicker basket marks the spot — Harry's death place. Fingers with cerise nails dip into the basket lifting biscuits, pâté, pickled onions, a brie wedge, apples, pork pies *et al* from its depths. I lie back on the patchwork blanket, enjoying the itch of the grass stubble beneath it, regularly eclipsing the sun with my beer bottle whose raised base becomes blazened. At the moment of death Harry lay like this. I trace his position mentally, my head on his and his hips under Andrea's. Far away in the Knuckles Range a sylph-like figure reads on a deep veranda, awaiting a turbaned postman. She is everywhere. Acutely acute. Yes, Sarah, as I promised, tonight.

89

Andrea plugs me with questions: how were the armies positioned? Where was the British headquarters? What Zulu regiments comprised what portion of the pincers? Enmeshed within my answers are snippets of Father's advice from our family visit and rehearsals of my answers to Sarah's demands for details. But surely you know, I implore Sarah as Andrea attempts to imagine the rout. She does but she doesn't. It is over a month since our last real rendezvous. How much her approach has changed: the compulsive outpourings have given way to persistent queries. No longer am I a mere receptacle: now I must answer unasked questions. To what end? is my repeated plea. Perhaps something will filter through during the journey to Ulundi. Perhaps it will provide the key.

Up we climb to Babanango, leaving the heat for the rarified nip of the highlands. Andrea's enthusiasm lessens as the Rover winds upwards. Trading stores, the hotel, police station, primary school, several churches, and the scattering of houses mark the watershed of her response. Inexplicably her enthusiasm has transformed into a sullenness which settles and consolidates as I nose for the coastal lowlands. To the accompaniment of Roberta Flack and Donny Hathaway singing, of all songs, 'You've Lost That Loving Feeling', we plummet, leaving the pines and mist for the pitch-and-roll of cane fields on the humid swell.

Always in the distance is the silver dome of the Ulundi memorial, erected in memory of the avenging of Isandlwana and to justify, among others, young Harry's death. To soothe the likes of Sarah. He died, of course, for Queen and Country, becoming a claimant to that corner of a foreign field, keeping it forever English. Had he not been one of many stacked beneath white cairns, he would probably have a personal, inscribed gravestone or, failing that, one of the many Here Lies A Brave British Soldier stones which scatter Natal. How people have squabbled for this lush belt between the Drakensberg and the sea: Boer-Black, British-Black, Boer-British — that eternal triangle — to our present complicated confrontation with its numerous fragments and divided loyalties. Like a jewel among the naggle of thorns, the growing dome sparkles as Andrea nods above a bestseller.

90

We arrive on schedule at three. The heat drums on the plain. Whydahs bob like pennons over the grass. Cicadas skirl. Volleys of sunlight ricochet off the silver dome. Waves shimmer beyond the formal garden as a pall of smoke spreads from the nearby kraals.

'Why,' asks Andrea, 'do all your memorials have to be phallic?' With my face hidden under the brim of my khaki hat, I walk on along the path between rows of aloes and Christ-thorn. Her sullenness is worse than ever.

'Like Kimberley?' I ask, signing my name in the visitors' book.

Away across the plain a heavily laden train labours towards Richards Bay. Beyond it, above the hotel, rise the KwaZulu Legislative Buildings. Workmen clamber between quills of reinforcing rods and jack hammers stutter like Gatling guns.

In the corner of the garden is the small British cemetery with its pale gravestones. I cross the gravel, retracing my steps of twenty years ago, and read the names. Beyond the War Graves Commission fence lie the Undi corps, the umXapho, the uDloko and the amaKwenkwe from the Gqikazi kraal, the umCijo and the uDududu, bundled beneath the thorn trees.

'A snake.' I hear Andrea shriek from near the memorial. The dark mamba, slung between the branches, eyes her beadily. She retreats into the dome and the snake flows away among the thorns.

'Where?' I ask.

'There.' She flicks her wrist towards the glare of the plain. Above her in the south passage is the inscription: In Memory Of The Brave Warriors Who Fell Here In 1879 In Defence Of The Old Zulu Order. It was, and still may be, the only memorial ever erected in honour of the Zulu nation.

It is cool inside.

'Were you bitten?' I feign concern. My gaze swings to a plaque.

A wood dove begins its lament: My mother is dead, my father is dead, all my relations are dead. . .

I find myself speaking: 'The British square formed here and the impi amassed out there on the plain. It is said that

91

just before the battle, as the armies were facing each other, a grey duiker broke cover and darted away down the corridor between the front ranks to cheers from the men. That incident has always been to me somehow symbolic.'

'Why?'

'As if the spirit were leaving the place.'

'Who was the British commander?' she asks, her profile reflected among the lettering on the brass.

'Lord Chelmsford.'

'Was he killed?'

'He died years later while playing billiards in his club in London.'

'Typical.' Beneath the long, fine bridge of her nose her nostrils dilate minutely.

I look out across the wide expanse. 'Chelmsford's army was encamped across the Umfolozi River. The day before the battle he sent a reconnaissance party up here onto the plain. The party was confronted by a band of Zulus and during the skirmish one trooper was shot dead and another wounded. They tried to save the wounded man but in the end he had to be left behind. That night the levies who were with the army near the river interpreted the songs which the Zulus were singing. The trooper, they said, had been handed over to the women and was being tortured by them. On the morning of the battle they found his body; his nose, right hand, ears and genitals had been cut off and, as was customary, his stomach had been slit open.'

. . . and my heart goes du du du du du.

'Mount the 17th' comes the cry. The infantry stops firing and begins cheering. Lord Chelmsford raises his field-glasses: the rout has begun: the lancers are skewering the fleeing warriors. Redemption at last.

The battle of Ulundi effectively marked the end of the Anglo-Zulu War. After the slaughter, the British troops razed the royal kraal at nearby Ondini. As the hundreds of beehive huts went up in flames, little did the redcoats realise that their attempt at obliteration was having the opposite effect.

Instead, the burning huts were transformed into kilns which fired the artefacts inside to a rock hardness. Today, when all that remains of the invaders are occasional rusted relics unearthed by herdboys, archaeologists, working under the aegis of the KwaZulu government, are rebuilding the kraal from its strong foundations: just beneath the surface of the gently sloping site is a Pompeii of fired floors and pot shards. Centuries hence, when even the largest artillery shells are dust, Ondini's remains will endure.

There are flags outside the hotel and an official portrait hangs in the foyer. Newspapers announce another bomb blast in Durban.

'Mr Wyatt-Edgell,' beams a receptionist.

'No,' I reply, startled, 'Colville.'

The ladies' bar is brimming with black civil servants drinking beer.

While the receptionists bustle I turn to Andrea: 'You must be careful of snakes at this time of the year. Especially mambas. The bites are extremely painful and invariably fatal. Shortly after being bitten you experience vertigo, difficulty in swallowing, increased salivation, slurred speech and drooping eyelids. After several hours your breathing stops.'

We follow the porter across the central patio to a row of bungalows.

After a cold shower, I lie back on the bed in my dressing-gown. Why call me Wyatt-Edgell, like the late captain, the only officer among the few British casualties, now the most senior participant in that little parade of stones beyond the monument? Why not anything but? My superstition demands exorcism so I pick up Madbolt and Shannon. Peering through a cloud of dispersing cheroot smoke, I begin to read his eulogy as Andrea disappears into the bathroom:

The country has lost a gallant officer. Heir-apparent to the barony of Braye, educated at Eton and Christ Church, Oxford, commissioned in the 17th Lancers, his loss will be sorely felt. When the enemy advance slackened, orders were received to strike at the wavering line. The lancers passed through the rear face of the square and advanced on the uNodwengo kraal where they wheeled right and approached a donga. Concealed in the grass on the opposite bank were some five hundred Zulus who poured in a considerable fusillade on the advancing men. This officer, gallantly leading his troop, was shot through the head.

93

Andrea returns, removes her dressing-gown and parts the curtains. Away across the plain crows are circling above the smoke from the kraals. The last rays of sunlight sheen the silver dome as a solitary duiker skips beyond the fence and dissolves into the gloom.

Andrea's voice: 'I'm not feeling well. I won't go with you to supper. I'll get something from room-service.'

So much for our big weekend.

Later, after a solitary meal, I cross the courtyard with its floodlit pool and enter the bar. Zulu War prints and imitation wood panelling. Settling on a stool, I order a J&B from the black barman whose white jacket has taken on a lemon glow in the muted lighting. He has a wide friendly face and his pouring of my drink has the deftness of a conjuror's performance; his hands pluck and swoop before the totted tumbler emerges from his fluttering fingers and lands gently on its coaster.

His teeth are a brief flash above his bow tie. We talk. I tell him of my interest in the Anglo-Zulu War and he expresses a fellow interest. Both of us, it turns out, lost forebears at Isandlwana.

'I have an assegai used in the battle.'

'How many British bellies did it slit open?' I ask, offering him a drink.

'Many.'

We laugh as he pours. I swivel and survey the crowded room: black men in white shirts and dark trousers circle tables littered with empties. The deep hubbub is stabbed occasionally by shrill laughter and I pick out several women. Light sprays from heavy pendulous shades and casts pools on whose surface fallen beer bottles bob like boats. It occurs to me that I am the only white and yet I don't feel the slightest hint of unease despite the conditioning of the system. In these pockets of multiracialism many people must realise that the bogey doesn't really exist. But there is always the chance of an unpleasant incident which colours future opinions.

Gradually the camaraderie envelops me. Both the barman and I have lost relatives on the same battlefield. All possibility

94

of animosity is drowned by the drink and the bond of common blood spilt not too recently. I go on to tell him that I have lost a brother in action in the operational area. Being an opponent of the system, Michael was, I explain, a double loser. He sympathises and I wonder if he has sons or brothers on the other side, but I don't ask.

Everything is slow and mellow and I can hear my voice: 'And what of Ulundi?' meaning the battle and not the emergent capital of KwaZulu. He tells me of the latter while seeing to the waiters' orders.

'There are too many problems to mention but I am lucky; I have a good job near home, a wife and children so the pain of the problems is less.'

'Another?' I offer.

'Thanks. Where's the woman I saw you with this afternoon, your wife?'

'She's feeling sick and has gone to bed.'

He tosses ice cubes into our tumblers. The squat goldenness of the J&B jumps to accommodate them. A dash of soda makes the cubes jingle. Everything is submerged and I yawn in the thickness.

Tots chase each other and the chatter softens. I am the last to leave; the bar door snaps shut behind me. Crossing the patio I disregard the dark dome above me with its sprinkling of stars. Immediate obstacles demand my attention. The room door is unco-operative but I master it and flounder through the darkness to the bed.

Andrea is half-awake, a form curled beside me. From within my fuddle, I reach out and begin caressing her thigh. It is warm and soft. My hand becomes more daring but is pushed away. Persistence is too exhausting. Instead, I begin thinking of Sarah and how I have abused her: this is *her* trip, yet she has been excluded. She is out there mad with expectation but this form beside me prohibits our meeting. Why is everything so complicated? Why is any progress so difficult?

My only comfort at Sarah's exclusion is that I have no answers to offer; I am drunk and ignorant.

16

Never give all the heart, for love
Will hardly seem worth thinking of
To passionate women if it seem
Certain, and they never dream
That it fades out from kiss to kiss;
For everything that's lovely is
But a brief, dreamy, kind delight.

W.B. Yeats. Never Give All the Heart

I have just received a scribbled note from Andrea; she won't ever be coming back; she and Willy Watkins are to announce their engagement. Her writing, never interesting at the best of times, looks more niggardly than usual. Her ballpoint traces the usual patter about our not having a future together and she offers her sincere apologies and best wishes for the future. We will, of course, remain friends.

Suddenly it all fits. I had obviously been on probation until our visit to Isandlwana, after which the decision went against me. Then followed our disastrous afternoon and evening at Ulundi. And so the jigsaw nears completion with only my pride hurt. But why Willy?

Strangely, I am not heartbroken. Instead there is a feeling of deep relief despite my earlier feelings of dependence. Rather solitude than stifling tension and silly outbursts.

On our return from Ulundi we stopped as planned at Fort Pearson where, during the war, a hawser was strung across the Tugela to Fort Tenedos on the other bank. Contemporary photographs show platoons of redcoats squashed shoulder-to-shoulder in the pont as it plied to and fro across the frontier. Somewhere in the camp above, Harry Colville scribbled his diary before his fateful return to his regiment in the central column en route to Isandlwana.

96

Leaving Andrea at the picnic site, I strolled down through the thorns and aloes to the brink; far below, the remainder of the once mighty river eased along its sandy bed towards its forested mouth. As at Isandlwana, I was acutely aware of Harry's presence. Apart from cosmetic changes — the depleted river, the swathe of sugar cane beyond the riverine bush — I was seeing it as he had. Sarah too was in the air. As if sensing my private elation, Andrea gave free reign to her rancour and I drove home with a mute beside me.

Rather Sarah than jet set banter and a draining quest for continuous fun. But there is also emptiness. No more weekends with a lithe and beautiful creature with splendid breasts and a mind uncluttered with complexities. No more natter about inanities. No more wafts of her particular scent, and brooding silences.

More time to brood and curse my foresight. To wonder at Sarah's choice and persistence. What messages are being sent by the cane? Time to hone my acuteness and learn more from my surroundings. With Moses and Brutus I have all the companions I need and in Sarah I have a soulmate. There is a sudden calmness about her now that Andrea and I are estranged. If Harry can be put to rest, there will just be the two of us. But first I must regain my ability to meet her face to face as it were. To honour my acceptance of her invitations. To cultivate an objectivity towards my surroundings and, with her help, to heighten my awareness. Only now do I realise that she may have the key to the cane's hummed riddle. Perhaps my linkage with Sarah has been ordained to enable my education in these prevalent but neglected messages. Perhaps she is my mentor whose task it is to assist me beyond mere sucrose content to the very pith.

Having decided to look again at the cane and to study it as something more than merely my source of livelihood, I attempt to tune in to its message: the soft sound which emerges from its leaves when they are hustled by the wind. Always there, and sometimes aided by the rasping of palm fronds and the lazy droning of bees, this gentle hum seems to beckon those who listen. Closer study reveals that its intensity has a highly sensitive fluctuation. Without the medium of trees or

97

grass or cane, the sound becomes so airy and faint that only sustained concentration reveals it. Where it originates remains a mystery but the cane fields seem to nurture and store it. Its strength in this vast reservoir of sound seems to be influenced by the cyclical growth pattern of the cane. Recently cut stalks have a subdued murmur before the pruned bases begin to sprout. Then the sound increases gradually until the cane reaches its prime and is heavy with sap. At this zenith it must be harvested or it begins to arrow, developing silky plumes, and declines in vitality.

Gradually, aided by much that I have gleaned unconsciously from childhood, I begin to hear the pure kernel of the sound which vibrates within the husk of the cane, wind, tree and insect sounds. Obviously this is what beckoned me during my odyssey home from farm school those many years ago.

The murmurings, it seems, are the simplest, most tangible, form of a vital sound movement in the upper air. Suddenly the puzzle half solves itself: there is a layered design of sound with its refinement increasing to a quintessential silence in the upper regions of the sky's dome. It is the lower gyres that I have heard occasionally as they settle on the cane. Why everything is suddenly revealing itself remains a mystery. Or a deception? Always here but only now appreciated is the cane. Perhaps I owe my new acuteness to Sarah now that Andrea is out of the way.

A man who is to me what his forebears were to mine; that is the riddle which plagues me.

The phone rings. It is Waterbosch Sugar Company with news of an explosion at the mill. Although the true extent of the damage has not yet been assessed, it appears that heavy machinery will have to be shipped out from England. Quotas will probably have to be reduced by as much as a third to accommodate this regretted annoyance. Security will be improved at the mill. A squad of black guards is being trained to man all entrances and all employees will be issued with identity documents. No one will be admitted without the necessary card. Apologies again but it is a sign of the times. My co-operation will be much appreciated.

I bumble through the morning, doing my rounds with feigned efficiency, giving orders like a tin god. Tractors and trailers lug their stack burdens, ranks of cutters advance, bands of togt women hoe water-grass and weeds between rows of shoots while among the stacks the Jerseys scrunch cane tops with that special tranquillity which so enchanted Andrea. The mechanic and his assistant rotavate a field in preparation for planting seed cane; stopping the Land Rover, I watch them, mesmerised by the systematic advance and retreat of the two tractors. Egrets pogo and circle through the dusty wakes as Brutus chases them, wading knee-deep through the mashed topsoil. I light a cheroot, draw deeply on it and relish its aroma while the muck seethes into me. An insect smudge on the windscreen hovers as the tractors move backwards and forwards through it like participants in a television game. Such precise tilling is always reassuring; it has an order which is inherently confident, raising two fingers at the uncertainties of the future.

At lunch I break my weekday quota of two beers and have another, toying with my curry before taking a siesta. After reading for several minutes, I am about to drift off when Moses appears with news that one of the rotavators has broken down and a new part is needed from Nonoti. With an alacrity that surprises me, I instruct the driver to slash the verges instead while I am away in town. The mechanic can repair the rotavator first thing tomorrow. Things should be back at full steam by mid-morning.

Remarkably, the part is in stock. Moving on to Hamid Patel and Son for tomorrow's rations, I avoid old man Patel, not feeling like one of his 'business discussions'. Leaving the Land Rover at the back of his warehouse to be loaded, I wander furtively through the shop itself, mingling with the crowd, hoping not to be spotted from the guard tower. Whirring fans attempt to move the steaming mugginess, but only ripple it, and the flies have that impudence which usually presages rain.

As I search a rack of spanspeks for one of the perfect soft-hardness, I notice in one of the mirrors which dangle awkwardly from the shelves of produce an Indian woman in a crimson sari. She is inspecting a pyramid of litchi sprays and every now and then an exquisitely delicate hand stretches out, opens, and like some fragile, fleeing animal, rustles about among the dry leaves. Several fine gold chains hang around her neck and in the slight dimple between one of her nostrils and the tip of her nose nestles a diamond. She peels off a litchi's horny skin, putting the soft, white, near-translucent fruit into her mouth. Her jaws move beneath the diamond and then the pip, brown and new-born glistening, appears from between her lips. She glances at me. Our eyes fuse momentarily and then her bright-eyedness quicksilvers away. She flits another glance; then she eases between the pyramids of fruit and out of the shop. Like a Hamelin child I follow. As she moves down an arcade through the throng, an image comes instantly to mind: a ruby, unearthed by a sudden storm, tumbling down a murky furrow.

The arcade activities seethe around me: baying fezzed dealers; a gargoyle rag-woman uttering an endless incantation for charity; a witchdoctor lurking in the dark doorway of a muti shop; a group of Zulu youths tapping their winkle-pickers in time with a kwela number, and several Indian women shopping serenely but now appearing dowdy beside my piper.

The close shadows open suddenly onto a courtyard cubicled with white sheets suspended from transverse washing lines, each wall palpitating gently in the heat like the gills of the Quarter. She vanishes among the palpitations. I sidestep through this brightly bleached maze and down a flight of uneven stairs. She looks up briefly from the lip of the gully and then vanishes into a tunnel of bamboos. Above us looms a mosque with mynahs chattering around the bulbs of its minarets. The muezzin appears, his shrill nasal cries exploding the birds into wild circling fragments.

The tunnel smells strongly of humus. At its head is a corrugated iron house. She slips inside. It is small and dilapidated with sagging shutters. There is a child-like quality about it, like an old doll's house abandoned in some forgotten nook of a huge garden.

Still uncannily bold, I ease open the door and step inside.

100

The room is white and sparsely furnished: several carpets partly cover the floorboards and a rosette of cushions encircles a vase filled with smouldering joss sticks. A single door leads deeper into the house; it is closed and on its face is a portrait of some bright-eyed goddess. Slowly the eyes arc leftwards and the woman appears, seating herself among the cushions. Light streaks slip haphazardly through the tired shutters, from time to time firing her diamond. (As with Andrea's ear-studs, remember?) I sit down beside her. She smells of some exotic fragrance just distinguishable in the fug of incense. Entranced, I stare at the glistening red dab on her forehead. We sit together in the quietness, becoming gradually aware of the emergence of some soft sitar music from behind the portrait. The sun drums on the roof as the incense tendrils dissipate upwards only to be blocked by the descending heat. I drown dreamily in the music, conscious only of her red dab shining down on me like a theatre light. I lie back, poised for vivisection. Lasered by her dab.

I hear her voice faintly from beyond the haziness. 'I know you.'

'Me?'

'Yes.'

'From where?' My lips are heavy and my tongue moves slowly like a wing of some ethered butterfly.

'From the farm.' The voice is soft and decades away.

'When?' I begin to feel uneasy. Perhaps this is a frame-up; she is some government stooge ensnaring me with a meticulously planned trifle, luring me to perform. My mind whirls: is there a hidden watcher? My recent estrangement from Andrea has made me easy prey. The curling smoke from the joss sticks plaits itself in the sitar music.

'Come, I'll tell you.' She leads me to the portrait and we enter the darkness behind the dab. It is black, and silent.

'When?' I repeat my question. My voice feels detached in the void.

'Remember,' she intones, 'the small blue corrugated iron house with its creepers and their golden and turquoise flowers and its ornaments and vases and the bright flags which fluttered above it while everything was tinkling?'

101

'The pooja house,' I exclaim, remembering it well despite the decades which have passed.

'Remember the Indian women who came out of the cane and the mangoes and avocados and disappeared into the house?'

'Yes.'

'Remember the person who, hidden in the rubber tree, watched them coming and going in the tinkling?'

'Yes. That was me,' I shout. The words reverberate in the hollow darkness. Sitar music filters into the silence. Incense smells permeate the blackness. Her sari sighs.

'I know,' her voice is calm and crystal clear, 'we used to watch you from inside.'

I am dumbstruck. The voice, sensing my sudden withdrawal, flows on with reassurances while I wallow in my guilt, apologising profusely, emphasising that I was merely a curious child who always wondered at their tinkling worship. While her attempts at solace continue, I rally but am again unnerved by associate questions. Are there others now watching me as I watch the steady decline? Am I perhaps a domino in a falling sequence? If so, when is it my turn to fall? Why has it been ordained that I am to be enlightened (if that's the right word) today? A hand settles on my shoulder as I jolt myself with the glibbest of answers: much of this is an illusion brought on by alcohol, the heat, and the trauma of separation from Andrea. From the time I was choosing spanspeks onwards, nothing is certain.

Somehow I find my way home. Parking the Land Rover in a shed, I walk across the lawn to the house. A sense of unreality exists. After a long shower which does nothing to clear my head, I have supper and move through to my study. Casting my mind back over the afternoon, I attempt to patch everything together. What you have read above is the best I can do. It won't become any clearer.

17

And so the plot thickens. With Andrea gone and Sarah still on the fringe, a strange Indian woman reveals that long ago she and her companions used to watch me from the pooja house while I, supposedly the active party, was spying on them. The more I observe the more I am observed. Anonymous saried figures among the avocados and mangoes become watchers whose object I inexplicably am. I can only ask what has become my perennial question. Why me? What makes me so interesting or boring that I demand scrutiny? And yet it seems that the more I attempt to solve that riddle the more elusive its solution becomes. Perhaps only from my perspective are Sarah and the Indian women riddles while from theirs I am the enigma.

But back to basics. Like a sleuth I must examine the facts.

Sarah: a late lissom beauty, daughter of a planter in the Knuckles Range, widow of the late Lieutenant Harry Colville, 24th Regiment (2nd Warwickshire), killed at Isandlwana.

Sarah: my spiritual (for want of a better description) companion, producer of the bushbaby ritual in which I perform, my mentor whom I now need more than ever.

Sarah: my partner with whom I trysted regularly before something intervened, making promises of 'tonight' come to nothing.

And the Indian women: delicate creatures transplanted among the cane fields and groves of mangoes and avocados; wives, relatives or friends of farm employees who, with red dabs on their foreheads, slipped into the pooja house behind the rubber tree for spells of worship or so it seemed.

Those are the available facts for what they are worth. Where from here? With progress snagged, I try for a lateral break. Is the arsonist, the 'parallel man' with an axe to grind, somehow linked to this? Can he be of assistance? Do I, in good police parlance, need him for questioning in connection with. . ? Is there a link, albeit extremely tenuous, between the sudden cooling of Andrea's ardour and the recent revelation that I was once the object of some Indian spying? Perhaps, tucked away somewhere, there is a voodoo doll bristling with pins.

I lapse into a spell of passivity, lulled by the seemingly impossible tangle of whys and wherefores ahead. Someone once wisely advised drifting but I now lack the courage, balking at the consequences. Instead I wallow in this interlude, relishing it more for its brevity. The heavy quietness is punctuated only by the thick tick-tock of the clock in the hall. Motes dance slowly in a ray of sunlight. I watch their random collisions, mustering just enough initiative to query the sequence. Perhaps thoughts have similar origins. I decide to summon a thought but realise that the act of summoning is itself a thought. The passivity returns and I am about to succumb when an incident that happened several years ago suddenly asserts itself. Dismissed then as merely a crankish intrusion, it now inexplicably needs consideration. The motes demand it.

Returning from the sheds at dusk one evening I noticed a figure blurred in the front doorway: Moses, I presumed, preparing the drinks tray. More blurring within the gathering darkness. Why, I asked myself, was Moses taking so long? A torch bobbed among the palms at the foot of the lawn: the nightwatchman on his beat. Brutus scampered down to join him. Was it Moses? Slowly the silhouette of a woman formed: she was tall and dark with unusually aquiline features. She met my annoyed stare directly. Her bearing was regal and aloof.

'What the bloody hell do you think you're doing?' I demanded in Zulu. She was bare footed and dressed in a hessian shift similar to those worn by the cutters. Her eyes scanned the night behind me; no answer. I reached for the door. It slammed in my face and was locked. I ran around the house; all the doors and windows were locked. I called the nightwatchman and told him of my encounter. His fury was immediate, his pride hurt. Moses slipped out of the shadows en route to the kitchen. Her head popped up like a jack in the scullery window and I pointed. She vanished. The curtains were drawn. We circled the house and she followed us, moving from room to room and peering out through the narrow partings in the drawn curtains. Whenever I pointed her out to the others, she vanished.

I instructed the nightwatchman to break the spare room window. He shattered the glass with his knobkerrie and we entered. We combed the house systematically. Two signs announced her presence: in my study the spotlight enhancing the Isandlwana painting was on, and the pot pourri jar on the spare room dressing-table, placed there at Andrea's insistence, was open and its contents strewn over the carpet. Again we tried all the windows and doors. All were locked from the inside.

I explained my encounter again. She was tall and slight. She was a black with the features of a white. Brutus barked outside; we moved to the window before remembering that everything was locked from the inside. The two men returned to their respective work: Moses to prepare the drinks tray and the nightwatchman back to his beat.

After supper I turned to Moses as I have done since childhood. What did he think? He had, he said, been thinking about the woman. He believed her now to be a spirit. As neither he nor the nightwatchman had seen her, she was clearly meant for me. She had come to tell me something but he could make nothing of the signs she had left. He suggested I consult a sangoma — something I have forgotten in the interim — to interpret the incident. I thought about it for several days and then decided not to pursue the matter. Nothing appeared to be stolen. Perhaps she was human and had merely slipped out of one of the shuttered windows, somehow pulling it to behind her. Although they hadn't seen her, both Moses and the nightwatchman were convinced of her existence. Unlike we whites, blacks seem better equipped to assess metaphysical goings-on. My apparent nonchalance seemed to impress them; a spirit enters my house and I am not sufficiently perturbed to turn to a sangoma for an explanation. I must indeed be brave. The spirits cannot touch me. The incident is to my advantage. Word spreads and over the years I catch snatches on the grapevine: that nkosaan is called by the spirits but he doesn't bother to answer; he must be happy in himself; they cannot lure him with promises; if the omen is bad, he doesn't care.

Conversely my visit to the sangoma after the recent arson attempt must have worked against me. A spirit enters my house and is disregarded but as soon as my cane is burnt I run off to the sangoma in search of a detection.

That is his Achilles' heel. His cane is his weakness. Burn it and you burn his life because without it he is nothing. Without his cane he will be forced to go. Attack him and he can shoot back but burn his cane and all he can do is try to extinguish the flames when you are far away.

I hope their deductions aren't as nit-picking as mine, and that they don't realise how much these intrusions and revelations erode my confidence.

As nothing resulted from my visit to the sangoma, it seems futile to return with questions of why the Indian women chose to counterspy. As Moses has mentioned repeatedly, the rural black doesn't understand the Indian and only resents the shimmy-shirted traders whose bargaining is so hard. Consequently they are merely caricatured and the blacks have little inkling of the workings of the eastern mind. Perhaps we whites are as ignorant. Perhaps we lack the capacity to understand other implantations on this alien landscape. Although we know no other, four generations still haven't brought us fully face to face with our surroundings; the hoopoe has nearly eclipsed the chaffinch but a feather of the latter remains.

Later, at dusk, I summon the bushbaby, playing a recital on my flute. After its dance it retreats into the branches to resume its silent vigil. The night sounds well up reassuringly and Sarah's arrival seems imminent. But inexplicably she breaks the pattern.

With no Andrea to cavort with and with Sarah's continued elusiveness plaguing me, I have no option but to turn to the gentle tumble of J&B for solace. After the few primers before and during dinner, I start my heavy tippling once Moses has gone. In a fug of cheroot smoke, the shelves of books in my study seem to weave in liquid. For fear of alarming Moses with my empties, I have taken to filling them with water and smuggling them into the Land Rover, later tossing them into the dam. Deep beneath the lily pads I am erecting an opaque green scaffold as a refuge for the shrapnel swarms of fingerlings and the slowly whipping eels.

Farm life continues, apparently smoothly. Black figures hack at the multitude of stalks, felling fields. Despite the reduced quota, squads of tractor-trailer tandems ply to and from the mill, having their loads plucked by the huge crane which hovers on runner-wings. Blades and crushers roar and snicker as the crane tosses the stalks onto the feeding belts.

Behind this frenetic activity are the back-up workers. In the yard the mechanic tinkers and in other fields women hoe between rows or scatter fertiliser onto the young shoots. Elsewhere other bands lay lengths of cane stalks in furrows, covering them with dark soil. In the stables the milking machine is dismantled for its weekly overhaul: glass jars and stainless steel pipes are scrubbed and run through with detergent and brushes. Throughout the garden, overalled gardeners squat with trowels, or power mowers into grassy inlets. Indoors, Moses, sporting a checked apron and a listing chef's cap, rolls and pummels as Rose glides through the rooms hoovering yesterday's dirt. Everything is as smooth as clockwork to the unpractised eye.

Desperate to maintain the tension, I carry out my daily rounds, meeting the indunas at the outside office after breakfast, handing out pills and bandages from the adjoining dispensary, and driving or walking incessantly, conjuring up that impression of omnipresence that keeps the ball rolling. To the workforce I must appear normal but inwardly I feel myself succumbing to an extreme ennui. All the unanswered questions have brought on nagging doubts which now plague me like furies. Why bother? increases in volume until it deafens me. Why record this stuff-up of a time when all is crumbling and no one is ever likely to find this neurotic scribbling?

This chronicle has reached a watershed. No longer is it an eager pointer dragging me by its leash. Instead, I am now the tired handler half-heartedly coaxing it off its haunches. Gone is the momentum. Instead I must drag myself to my desk for

107

a few scribbled lines before the J&B takes over. The progress is painfully slow. Even as I write these words, I stumble.

The tense trick I mentioned earlier has simplified: what I am now saying is no longer the condensation of three tenses into one. Instead of describing past happenings in the present, my words are now of immediate relevance. The lethargy has set in; my fingers whorl slowly as I use my free hand to pour another tot. The warp is now altered: you are being confronted by my present slowness. If you relate to me you are as slow as I am. The whole happening-writing-reading show is barely on the road.

Outside, the cane is growing imperceptibly. Cropped bases become shoots which struggle upwards, sprouting leaves and swelling with sap. Charts in my office near the dispensary indicate the cutters' next move and all the fields must be razed before the tell-tale emergence of arrows from the growing tips. With all the stalks safely delivered and somewhere being converted into princely sums, the bases undergo their transformation. Eventually, repeated ratooning takes its toll and the field must be ploughed. Stalks of eager seed cane from the experiment station replace the jaded ratooner. And so the cycle continues endlessly, the snake swallowing its tail, until the reason for turning is lost. Without impetus even the smoothest wheel slows and stops.

Monkey chatter. Mobs of the bandarlog have appeared from nowhere and are trapezing up the gully below the house. Beneath the swaying tree-tops is the devastation. Eggs and fledgelings are snatched between the frantic dive-bombings of the screeching parent birds. Fruit fights create gaudy carpets in the undergrowth, each frilled with gobbets of cane. The furies pause long enough to allow filterings of the childhood order demanding culling. The least I can do is adopt the role of the leopard and try to keep what is left of the balance. An activity with an immediate visual reward would, I am sure, be recommended by any doctor who discovers this scribbling behind the bottles in the cellar.

18

For the last half hour a squalling cry has repeatedly interrupted my laboured attempts to fill this page. Surpassing all other distractions — the shrilling crickets, the mellow glow from my tumbler, Brutus's snuffling on the veranda — it has forced itself onto the page, wedging in between my present low and later's surprises. Now that it has gained admission, I am its host. Courtesy moves me to the window. The garden is dark and jumbled with the strange humps of shrubs and borders. Down near the stables, beyond the tennis court, the nightwatchman's torch bobs reassuringly. Would intruders prudently avoid him or is he lumped in with me? Or is he in cahoots with them? Something skittles the flatcrown leaves. A blob scampers from branch to branch. The bushbaby. It seems unusually animated, almost demanding a recital. I need no coaxing. Widening the happening-writing void, I collect my flute and slip outside.

Tonight's performance is the most vital to date. After several introductory trills, I become suddenly transformed into the most eager accompanist, obsessed with the possibility of another tryst with Sarah. Like an ecstatic Pan I cavort around the wicker chair as the bushbaby hops and shuffles. On and on I play, oblivious of appearing mad to the nightwatchman should he be confronted by another example of the umlungu's strangeness. Stuff it all. I am bursting with an irrational enthusiasm. My wild abandon stops at nothing.

Then, the bushbaby is gone. Rushing inside for a bottle of J&B, I return to the veranda and begin my vigil umbrellaed by the dark looming of the flatcrown. Soon I feel Sarah's presence as she moves up from the gully and through the amatungulu. For the first time in weeks I can hear the cane clearly. Sarah ascends through its hushing.

Trying hard to contain my emotion, I greet her and ask the purpose of her visit. So much has been happening and I

109

am confused and in need of reassurance. Does she have any answers? She ignores my question and instead begins a hurried monologue:

'Mama, Maisie and me within the Sigiriya cave watch frescoed processions of olive and honey women slip along the walls, growing from the darkness. Strange beauties with swelling breasts held snugly in transparent bodices above hips half lost in clouds: breasts like bowling woods with circular bias nipples. Fifteen centuries old, they have withdrawn into the stone and gaze heavy-lidded at us. All captured in time. Some proffer full-blown lotuses from tiny hands. Why lotuses? We pledge to find out. Pink bodies in cotton frocks, we scan these reflections, Mama's closed parasol a wilting lotus. Gold and emeralds flash from amulets, bangles, ear-rings, and tiaras pierced by aigrettes. All heavy with symbolism but written by the sittara in a language foreign to us. These figures gaze back at our pale pinkness, possibly wondering who and why. Local colour versus our pastels like you and the pooja house portrait. Maisie whispers: their noses are like yours; I blanch, then glow. Native me, an apsara cut off by whiteness. What, I wonder, would my dear Harry think of this parade? My Paris forced to choose. But now so far away on some senseless mission to crush the Zooloo.

'I can see the sittara, a little yellow man in a saffron robe, his delicate hand guiding the brush through its slow curls, licking colour and form onto the dull stone. Hours and hours of meticulous toiling driven by unstinting belief. Slowly, lick by lick, the lush women emerge, offering their wares to their creator as he offers them. Here on the walls he captures his belief, making it endure beyond himself, leaving his inspired handiwork for all to see and wonder at. And so the women live on, taking with them the little shaven monk and his impetus.

'Mama has caught it: "These girls mirror a particular belief at a particular time. Who, I wonder, were his models and why did he paint them as he did? We can marvel but only someone then could get the same effect."

110

'Rooted in their time, they stare timelessly as we drift past. 'And then homewards along the Kandy road which whips about through the forest teeming with wanderoos. Villages burst from the undergrowth as we scatter passers-by who bow with old-world courtesy in time with Maisie's mutterings: "I wish they wouldn't fawn so." Presently we descend into a grove where a river has strung a series of pools. Women are bathing, their hair coiled on their heads. Dark, graceful creatures who make me feel dobbinish. They watch as we pass, a procession against the muddy banks. Women like, but unlike, those at Sigiriya. More real but less so. Less enduring but the real thing.

'Bumping through a cutting and around a corner in the bullock cart, we find the road blocked. Catheramatamby calls for a thoroughfare. The mob moves, spokes turning and revealing the hub. A monk is lying on threads of blood, his saffron robe polka-dotted. A shaven head, hands and feet protrude from the swathe. Mama instructs Catheramatamby to find out. Excited babblings reveal that the victim, a passing scholar, has been attacked by a wild animal. A leopard perhaps. Or a wild boar. Is he dead? No. They are waiting for a policeman and a doctor. Can we help? No.

'For the remainder of the journey we talk very little. Blood is a dampener. Maisie utters the usual sentiments but canny Mama is more inquiring. Why, she wonders, was the little traveller wounded at that spot? Was he en route to the caves or returning from them? Inevitably, doubt is the only answer. Should he die, the faith on which he travelled will keep moving. That part of him remains. And yet who is to say that the other will really be gone? We lapse into silence. I marvel now at her acuteness. So close and yet so far.

'It is dusk when we churn through the drift below the coolie lines and scrunch up the drive to the house. Papa is waiting on the veranda. We alight. Instead of approaching and kissing us as is customary, he waits where he is. Mama is called and they whisper. I am called and settled in the old armchair with the faded floral pattern. A *Blackwoods* magazine is open on the arm; I implore both pages to negate my hunch. Papa holds an envelope. His hand is shaking. Between

111

his fingers is the official stamp.

'My poor Harry . . .'

At the mention of his name she vanishes, leaving a soundless echo which suggests a great urgency. Bursting with questions, I call out to her but she has withdrawn beyond the cane. There is none of the usual calmness; instead the air is restless with a strange electricity. The cane's hushing is inaudible again. Somewhere, but only just, is the hum.

Glad at her return but peeved by my role as a passive listener, I bumble to bed. What of her visit to the sacred caves and the goring of the travelling monk/scholar on the day that she heard of Harry's death? Is she merely unburdening herself or do I have something to learn from her Ceylonese parable? Her photograph peers down from my dressing-table with infuriating aloofness.

From my bedside table I pick up a pen and paper and, cheating slightly of necessity, record in the present my recent meeting with Sarah, splicing it in between the ninth- and tenth-last sentences.

What do I really think? Perhaps, like her mysterious arrival, her inexplicable departure was preordained: the thread cut. How do I feel now? I demand of myself, wanting an immediate response, wanting to include it before it cools and undergoes the inevitable revision. My answer: happy at these added lines, but otherwise saddish, with a strange sense of finality.

When assessed by this immediate criterion, the greatest part of this account is cheating so note this slight warp into the future. I write 'I go to sleep' as I switch off the light. A buff-spotted flufftail hoot-whistles intermittently and a mosquito whines near the ceiling: the former darting about deep in the cane; the latter tracing its delicate thread along the cornice. A brief pause as I put down the pen and paper. Again the gap widens because the action of setting aside the necessary instruments cannot coincide with its recording. Such are the limitations of illusion although it often holds greater truths. Reality remains just off centre.

It is at times like this that I feel the loss of Andrea most. With my tendency to bog down, I need her lightness. Her frivolities are fun without questions. The unseen is another world whereas a giggle is of this one. Perhaps she will return; her nature needs a dark foil and will fizzle beside weakness.

19

Breakfast. Moses enters with my scrambled eggs. He has news. On his way home on Friday afternoon, remembering that I had had no luck as yet in tracking down the arsonist, he decided to visit the sangoma on my behalf. It was dusk when he reached her cave above the Tugela and he was in a hurry to be done before darkness set in. While waiting for the umfaan to emerge and ask his business, he was startled to hear a jabbering from a cluster of roots suspended from the quoin of the cave's entrance. Calling him by name, it said that he had been expected and gave instructions to tell me that I was about to make a breakthrough. Falling to his knees, he waited for more but lacked the courage to question the voice. A short silence was followed by indignant squeaking from the bats. In a muck sweat, unable to control himself, he had sprinted away along the path to the trading store, oblivious of his gammy leg. That was all the news he had. I should be patient because we will catch the culprit.

I thank him very much, stressing how much I am heartened by the news. I will be alert for clues. A man who is to me what his forebears were to mine. I am no closer now than in the beginning but I must, on instructions, persevere.

Realising how in awe many blacks are of sangomas, I appreciate the extent of Moses' gesture. Nobody else, I am convinced, would have done something so courageous for me. Consequently, I trust him more than I trust anybody else. It occurs to me that I should perhaps alter my will and leave the farm to him rather than my cousin, a pallid youth in Ireland. Although this country's laws preclude a black from owning land of this sort, everything could be sold and he be given the proceeds. Merely because Walter Colville's father happened to be my father's younger brother, why should he be given such a handout? After all, I have met him only once; while a student in Dublin I travelled with my relatives to Coole

114

Park, once Lady Gregory's home and a refuge for Irish literati. We picnicked beside the lake. The sole beneficiary of my will was then a pimpled teenager with a love of model bi-planes. Accompanying him to the water's edge was a yellow Tiger Moth with streamers of dried glue smudged down its struts. A vestige of an earlier stage, it never left his side.

That visit, like several others, remains crystal clear. Last year Andrea and I toured Ireland. After an exhaustive round of my old haunts in Dublin — an ultimately depressing venture because that past ambience cannot be reconjured — I dragged her on a treasure hunt clockwise through the counties. Among the catalysts was my desire to see whether Corsehill, the home of my great-great grandfather, still existed. What had further fanned my curiosity was the acquaintance I had made several months previously with Sarah, whose Harry had spent his childhood there.

One afternoon, after a boozy lunch with an old Trinity friend then farming near Gort, we set out in a hired Hillman for our hotel. It was drizzling and Andrea, with all the languor of a sloth, was, characteristically, lying across from the passenger seat with her head cupped in my lap. On we raced through the haze of wetness, her breathing lapping gently against the hem of my jacket.

A sign: Coole Park. The sudden memory rush of those other visits there as a student and a desire to see it again with that slice of time removed.

I turned into the tightly-knit avenue of holm-oaks, accelerating within the vault: wreaths of twisting branches; a maze of confused windings. I snapped on the headlights and they probed the mad matting and slipped on, leaving the witches' dream in its darkness. On to where the house had stood before the gobeen men demolished it for the price of its stone. Only the remains of the outbuildings traced themselves in the grass. Worlds away were Robert Gregory's childhood and the visits of Yeats, AE, Synge, O'Casey and Martyn who once engraved their initials on the copper beech in the walled pleasure-garden. Mercifully the tree still stood, protected by railings. Mumblings from Andrea got reassurances and she dozed off again.

115

Back onto the main road and sharp right. I accelerated, whistling quietly to the accompaniment of the swishing tyres and the slip-flop of the windscreen-wipers. Fumbling with a map on the console, I peered for an alternative route to the hotel, in a hurry as night was approaching and the rain seemed to be intensifying. Finding a short cut, I raced through stone-walled undulations, surprising cottages and the remains of big houses as they withdrew into groves or scanned from hillocks.

At a crossroads in a valley a herd of Friesland cattle milled across the road, causing me to brake, then edge forward, nudging through them. Suddenly, inexplicably, I looked to my right and saw imposing stone gates patterned with ivy. Just visible between the runners was the name — Corsehill. Casting my eyes up the wandering drive at the silhouette of crumbling ramparts — more relics of an extinct order — I was filled with wistfulness. Just visible among the heaped masonry were several arches through which what was left of the light was glowing eerily.

So here was where Harry Colville spent his childhood. Among these solemn dripping oaks, I told myself, he and my great grandfather probably hunted while on holiday from Charterhouse. Sarah enthused about his markmanship. There is a photograph taken somewhere in Ceylon of him posing proudly beside two axis rams. Little did he know then what was in store for him.

Michael was always a better monkey culler than I was. He once bagged two bulls with a single shot of the Holland & Holland. Little did he too know of what lay ahead. But no more or less than I do now.

Asking an old herd who was chivvying the cattle across flag-stones into a milking parlour whether I could visit the house I was told there was nothing left to see. My query as to whether he remembered anyone who had lived at Corsehill was answered with a wry smile and what sounded like the mouth-ing of the word Colville. Yes, he nodded, pointing up at the ruins, long ago a lady lived there alone but when the troubles came she left. He was a child then but he remembered her well. She was very beautiful and wore dresses of silk. There were parties once but that was long before. On the night they burned down the house he was standing there with his mother. He gestured across a stream to a sloping field. The glow was so bright that it was like noon on a summer's day. You could see everything. People came from miles around to watch the flames.

Will this house have as big an audience? Will hordes congregate to watch Rangoon House become a pyre? Perhaps.

But now here I am, as introspective as ever, with an elderly Zulu, a gentleman's gentleman if I can be so presumptuous as to assume the former description, as my only confidant. While most whites look naturally to others of their kind for the discussion and mulling over of thoughts and experiences, they fail to realise that much is lost because our grafting in African soil takes generations, even centuries, before deep tap-roots are established. Until then our exclusive appreciation of our surroundings must remain fragmentary. Conversely, confiding in someone like Moses gives me that local dimension but in turn loses the acuity achieved when there is a cultural common ground.

If, however, Moses is my mentor or father of sorts, the flat-crown off the front veranda is my mother. From as early as I can remember she has, with her looming, provided me with protection. Like a chick, I have sheltered under her wings. She suspended the sock containing a tired corkie which I further assaulted to break in my linseeded bat. She provided clambering and building sites for Michael and me in our respective arboreal stages. During my drink rituals at dusk and at noon during weekends, she is in quiet attendance. At her bidding perhaps the harbinger emerges before our performance and afterwards the star withdraws into her darkness. Like an anchor to which the house and its inmate are secured, she steadies us through the buffetings of the present deterioration. No matter what the radio or newspapers say, she is there with her gentle swaying and soft dove chorus.

Should a bolt of lightning split and upend her, I would be exposed to the elements. Unprotected, I would retire indoors, emerging only at the beck of the cane to ensure that the farm work continues. Like a visitor I would go ashore only for brief periods, soon returning aboard.

117

Why, doctor, is it that I need these surrogates? Why must the creator of the charred sheets in the asbestos cylinder harp on about belonging? Doesn't the fact that this farm has always been my home give me a real claim to it? Perhaps a small legacy will see Moses into comfortable retirement while I shed myself of this hereditary burden and take old man Patel's advice, globe-trotting away from my doubts. Perhaps a stateless life provides the fluidity to endure. Perhaps, but you know how hamstrung I really am. Only one thing is certain: doubts are a privilege. When the shit hits the fan there will no longer be time for them.

20

I squat deep in the maidenhair in the gully, resting the Holland & Holland across my knees and scanning the slowly swaying canopy of leaves for the sudden shudder of monkey movement. Below me sounds the stream's fern-filtered tinkle and through a gap in the swaying branches a black-shouldered kite high-circles in the dome. I rub my thumb across the safety catch, enjoying the feel of its slight serrations. A brief shaking among the upper branches. I fix my attention on a patch of leaf shadow, imagining several monkey forms among the dapples. Nothing. Two barbets perform noisily in a large fig. I watch their animated bobbing, then lower my gaze down the length of the tree to its fibrous roots which dangle like pizzles from the bank.

A tortoise scuffs slowly about among the rotting fruit. I change position and it hesitates and half retracts itself before re-emerging and continuing. A scraping in the fern beside me: another tortoise appears and begins to walk bow-leggedly towards the fig. The forager turns, wide-eyed. Gulping convulsively they approach each other. On confrontation, a bout of butting and shoving begins as each tortoise attempts to dislodge and overturn its opponent. Both are repeatedly knocked onto two legs but on each occasion the flounderer manages to regain his balance. I watch their clumsy resolute combat, spellbound by their doggedness.

Eventually, the forager dislodges the intruder and, ramming forward under his belly, prises him onto his shell. He flails the air, rowing among the rotting figs, attempting unsuccessfully to gain leverage. I refuse to intervene. The forager, his throat palpitating wildly, studies the intruder's predicament for several minutes, then moves across and bumps him back onto his feet. Overwhelmed by this sportsmanship, I ignore the monkey chatter above me. The intruder promptly leaves the clearing and disappears into the ferns. Delight bursts within me at this chivalry. I am tempted to yell inwardly for Sarah but realise its futility. I yell for Andrea but there is no reply. I envisage her response: open laughter and dimples. But that is all gone now.

Shuddering branches; I snap the catch, swing the gun upwards and squeeze one trigger; burst: leaf fragments float downwards. Another shudder; burst: more confetti. Silence.

I release the two cartridges. Bugger; it is years since I have wasted such easy shots. I reload the shotgun, light a cheroot and lie back like a leopard among the ferns. The canopy rocks gently behind an aromatic screen of cordite and cheroot smoke. The sound of the stream mingles with the slow rocking movement, lulling me into a state of deep passivity. Beyond the rise and fall of my chest is the wild tangle of foliage — confusion laced with a meticulous delicacy. My stare reveals an intricate order: each liana is perfectly festooned; branches mesh with their neighbours; fungi patterns suggest messages. All are peacefully bound for humus and regeneration. Life sprouts from mounds of death. While we gnaw ourselves with questions of the after-life, these supposedly inanimate objects cycle perfectly.

Colour-flashes in an umdoni announce a purple-crested loerie which hops through the branches, eyeing me quizzically. How must I appear to it? A pale branched form holding a twig of smouldering tinder? The animal from up the hill? Or merely an indistinct object of curiosity? I draw vigorously on the cheroot; the bird watches my smoke-signals and glides off into the greenness beyond the stream. Reappearing in the fig, it resumes its scrutiny.

Singing sifts down through the cane and bush from the road beneath the house. Turning onto my stomach, I press-up from the ferns and leave the gully, climbing towards the voices up a steep path used by black women to collect firewood. I allow them to take only dead branches; the cutting down of healthy trees warrants immediate dismissal for both the woman and her family. Consequently, the bush is intact. Only the monkeys disrupt the balance and have to be culled. Only they disrupt the harmony. I adopt the leopard's task to keep things on the level. The singing is clear and vibrant. A party or some religious gathering, I presume, changing venue. Reaching the road, I slip into a copse of aloes, waiting for the celebrants to round the corner, wanting to watch them unobserved.

They appear: a procession of black women led by a man. He utters a resonant drone upon which the feminine voices dance. Holding a staff vertically in front of him with his purple robe hanging in dewlaps from his extended arms, he shuffles forward, followed by the throng of similarly dressed women with their robes in disarray and their breasts exposed. The feminine voices rise from a rich ringing to a teetering screech at which individual women trill and whoop until they subside, bringing down with them the body of the sound, settling it again before sufficient vigour is accumulated to launch another jagged arc. This undulation is punctuated by thudding tom-toms played by two adolescent girls who, with their faces daubed with ochre mud, jink frantically down the flanks of the body. On drones the baritone studded with drumming; up rises the wailing, tightening into a screech, oscillating erratically, then subsiding.

A tall woman breaks free from the column and, shrilling, hula-hoops towards my hideaway. Her eyes are filmed; her mamba-tongue curls and flickers; she contorts wildly, her small breasts tremoring from her torn robe; then returns to the creeping morph.

Both frightened and fascinated by this African bacchanalia, I crane between the succulent spines, ignoring my inner conflict: my white conditioning implores me to reject this apparently pagan rejoicing while I magnet towards it. From the celebrants radiates a searing energy and I can see in each of them some of Andrea's vitality coupled with that hysteria so apparent in my photograph of Sarah. Both beckon me from each woman's frenzy but as master of the estate I restrain myself and, crouching in the aloes, follow the bacchantes along the side of the hill and into the forested tunnel.

At lunch, over curry and an array of sambals, I listen beyond the intonation of the radio news to the memory of that strange singing. Brutus bursts from the hydrangeas beyond the pool and pads wearily to the veranda where he

121

collapses. The regularity of his panting is interrupted by sudden sucks in a vain attempt to vacuum slobber; then back to the rhythm. Each dancer performs but the tall breakaway demands attention. Her detachment from the party and sally towards me has skittled my thoughts. Images flash until I find myself thinking of the intruder of several years ago. Immediately, it dawns on me that they look identical.

As during my encounter with the pooja house woman, I am dumbstruck. Somebody somehow is contriving a drama in which I, the fool, am playing a pivotal role. First I am lured with baits and then the tables are turned. That somebody knows my foibles well; each trap is so ingeniously set that I am oblivious of being ensnared until sometime later (decades in the case of the pooja house plot, although that tête-à-tête may also have been a charade).

What has just ended is a new version of an old scene. Unwittingly I was putting on a performance for the bacchantes and not vice versa. Like an ecstatic spectator in the front row, she was writhing at my crouching. As when I spied on the pooja house, I have become the watched. When this riddle will be solved is impossible to guess. One day, perhaps years or decades hence, if ever, things will filter through. I may, however, even pre-decease the solution's arrival.

Whose pawn am I? I list the possible culprits. Is this some occult magic of Sarah's? Alternatively, is the intruder-cum-celebrant an agent for the sangoma? Perhaps the hag is in need of more whisky and is goading me into another appointment. Did Moses' recent visit re-open my case? Or perhaps this subtle intimidation is part of the inevitable rejection: Whitey go home. But this is my home, I counter, demanding a different tack. Whitey go back to where your ancestors came from.

Somehow circumstances have shuffled the pack against me and I can only admit defeat. Or, are these all mind games, frantic manifestations of my growing paranoia? Perhaps the latter, but my very consideration of the possibility presupposes some sanity. If I were too far gone, I wouldn't dream of illness. As you know, only the sane fear insanity. The insane don't even consider it.

2 1

'Apparently random scenes — both normal and conjured from the void — can, through their particular selection and shuffling, reveal crucial truths to those in search of guidance.'

That sentence confronted me like a neon sign during my recent browsing through *The Riddles Of The Paranormal* by Theodore Browka, a quaint tome which I had sent to me after my meeting with the sangoma. Years ago my father established contact with several antiquarian booksellers in London who have continued to send their catalogues to this address. With the local dearth of interesting old books, I order from them regularly.

According to Browka, an apparent adept of the paranormal, there must be method in all these mad happenings. Sarah's monologues, as much as the many mundane and unusual happenings which have confronted me, including those which in turn have introduced their own siblings, must, like the tossed coins or cast yarrow stalks of the I Ching, be an ordered glimpse of some cosmic pattern.

Like everyone else I am part of a play whose script is being written as I live it. An apparent hotchpotch of forces from my — and others' — past, present and future continually alters my course whose direction can, so Browka says, be known prematurely by an ingenious short-circuiting.

Much of my present predicament, including my laboured attempts to press on with this chronicle, stems, as far as I am able to determine, from a desire to take the crucial step out of this stifling decay. Like a master driver, I am listening carefully to the engine's revs, waiting for just the right pitch to jerk the lever and change gear without using the damaged clutch. Consequently, I must keep attuned to the hum, monitoring its cadences for just the right moment to act.

As you can see, I am lucid again. My lunchtime panic was nothing; a mild aberration. Normal coincidences are being rigged by me. Lookalikes become the same person. The intruder was really nothing more than a burglar and this morning's celebrants were merely zealous members of some Zionist sect. I did spy on the Indian women long ago but they never saw me. My recent tête-à-tête among the joss sticks was nothing more than a vivid dream motivated by my need to exorcise my childish guilt. Now that I have made a clean slate of it, the naughty boy bit can be laid to rest. Knowing this, I can continue, except for one hindrance: Sarah's final monologue highlighted Harry's death and I must relive the actual circumstances.

For what happened we must turn to an account given years after the battle by a Zulu induna of the iShudu section of the uMbonambi Regiment. A historian, scouring Zululand for survivors of the battle and recording their experiences, had found the elderly veteran in a kraal in the Qudeni district. Never prepared for publication, the scribbled pages yellowed and foxed in the Durban archives until their editing and inclusion in Madbolt and Shannon's fourth edition inadvertently supplied our puzzle with a vital jigsaw piece which was so nearly lost. I quote:

When the uMbonambi and the inGobamakhosi crested the saddle between Isandlwana hill and Stony Koppie, all those who were going to survive had already escaped. For the remainder, it was every man for himself. A rush of refugees, some on horseback and others on foot, retreated towards Rorke's Drift or Helpmekaar. Among them the induna noticed two officers, one brown haired and the other fair (subsequently identified as Lieutenants Colville and Hamilton respectively) attempting to gallop around the vanguards of the uNokenke and uDududu as they emerged from around the mountain, encircling the British left flank in a classic pincer movement. As yet uninvolved in the fighting, these youngbloods, eager to wash their spears, surged towards the two subalterns. Lieutenant Hamilton kept firing his revolver and Colville had a sword with which he slashed at his attackers. Realising that their escape was blocked, both reined in and attempted to return to the foot of the hill where a group of men (the remnants of Lieutenant Pope's company) had rallied for a last stand.

As he turned, Hamilton was dragged from his horse and butchered, but Colville, slashing desperately with his sword, managed to retreat some fifty yards before his horse was brought down. Preoccupied with the eager youngbloods behind him, he ran towards the rallying point, oblivious of the induna who, having been wounded earlier in the battle, was limping across from the burning wagons. Struggling through the mêlée, Colville pivoted, slashing at his pursuers, gashing their leader at the very moment that the induna plunged an assegai into the nape of his neck. Swivelling with the impact, Colville grabbed the shaft and with supreme effort almost succeeded in pulling out the assegai (a footnote records that at this point in his story the induna writhed in pantomime of the officer's movements) before someone finished him off.

I study his portrait, trying to imagine the protrusion of the assegai blade from his Adam's apple, but the immaculateness of his dress tunic quashes my mind-conjuring. Instead, the oval photograph remains defiantly sacrosanct.

Luckily the long gestation of the induna's account spared Sarah the details of her Harry's death although the imagined horrors of his disembowelment haunted her forever. Perhaps, on her death, she got it all first hand. If so, why did she pester me for answers? Apologies for yet another question; it was meant to be rhetorical; I know it has no answer. Anyway, things must be easier with them both beyond. Both in a common medium, as it were. My assistance was needed only for those snippets which had inexplicably remained obscure.

Michael's death, as far as is known, was less spectacular. Some weeks after the news had been broken to them by a chaplain from the local command, Mother and Father made contact with Michael's section leader — a miner's son from somewhere in the Orange Free State — who, in a long and barely legible letter, told of the circumstances. After a brief and successful contact with Swapo forces in some hamlet in southern Angola, the South African troops began mopping up in the vicinity. While Michael's section was scouring a field of pecan nut trees, a single shot rang out. The bullet passed through his neck, severing his spinal cord. Death was instantaneous; the family doctor endorsed this when told the facts. That was some solace. Michael's incensed companions then apparently conducted a brief follow-up operation but found no one.

His body was eventually flown home and he now lies just within the fence of the little cemetery of St John's Church,

Umsundu. Flanking him are other family members; only feet away through the few rusted strands are the forebears of the Ramlakan family who have long been gardeners here. This afternoon, while I was working on this, chief gardener Teddy Ramlakan appeared suddenly among the azaleas at the foot of the lawn like a shadowy figure in a Rousseau painting, only to vanish again, trowel in hand.

Fatigue settles. All this talk of death is debilitating. J&B is no longer enough. I must seek refuge in sleep. I collapse on my bed and am soon gone, while my mind, like an engine with pre-ignition, runs on in a restless limbo, sparked off no doubt by these martial musings and the registered letter. Collected by Krish (who signed on my behalf) in Nonoti, the khaki envelope arrived with my afternoon tea. One glance was enough. The contents soon confirmed my suspicion: B Company, Natal Fusiliers will be doing a ninety-day camp in the operational area, beginning next month. Reply immed-iately. Like a meditator bothered by an intrusion, I willed it away, tucking into the tea and cakes. Briefly forgotten, the depressing prospect has now returned, triggering thoughts of disparate incidents from my national service, juxtaposing them, placing me in a sequence that never really was but which, through some unconscious selection (Browka again), probably has something to say.

The four of us — Mad Dog, Gosling, Heksdokter and my-self — are in a tent in the bush somewhere on the border. Defending our country from the enemy and ourselves from the omnipresent heat, snakes, mosquitoes, scorpions, and that treacherous incubus, that harbinger of madness, bush fever, which lurks in our isolation, ever eager to enter our heads. Four of us in a tent among many tents, lolling half-naked on our beds among a litter of equipment. Dying of boredom and the heat, compulsively cleaning our rifles: removing their heavy dewlap-magazines, hounding the cinna-mon dust from the crannies and slashing our pull-throughs at the flies.

Forever waiting for orders.

Heksdokter, like a corpse in mid-ascension, detaches him-self from his bed and slouches resignedly to the middle of the

126

tent where he begins to dig a large hole with his bayonet.

'Hey, no shit in the tent,' quips Mad Dog from his cubicle of groundsheets.

'Then what you doing here?' Heksdokter smiles smugly at his glib reply.

'My National Service.'

With an air of bored resignation, Heksdokter fiddles about with his toothbrush and toothpaste, eventually spitting and retching into the hole. He squats beside it and, transfixed, watches the slow seeping of his spittle into the hard ground. Finally, satisfied that all but a white foam has been absorbed, he scuffs back the loose earth and slaps it flat with a sandal before returning to his bed where he again collapses.

'I would like to propose that we pray for Heksdokter's teeth. Any seconders?' Mad Dog's obsession — the tent constitution, the democratic treatise governing tent activities.

'Yes,' quavers Gosling in Afrikaans. Being a government supporter, he loves politics. He refuses to speak English although he is the only Afrikaner in the tent. We voted that he should at least speak some English but he refuses, pointing out that bilingualism is an entrenched clause. Heksdokter scoffs that he should only look back several decades to see how much his government honours entrenched clauses. This infuriates Gosling and while he raves that Heksdokter is subversive and an English enemy of the State, Heksdokter recites his usual refrain: 'If we should die, think only this of us, that there was once three-quarters of a foreign tent that spoke forever English.' Then adds: 'Anyway, I'm not bloody English, I'm an English-speaking South African.'

'Nimbus?' asks Mad Dog.

'Against.' I usually vote against.

I work in league with Heksdokter, ensuring that nothing is passed of which we disapprove. This riles Mad Dog, the chief proposer of motions.

'Two for, two against.'

Heksdokter puts down *The Hound of the Baskervilles* and lifts his section of the tent flap.

'Let us pray,' begins Mad Dog. 'Dear God, we give thee humble and hearty thanks for our teeth but call upon thy infi-

127

nite power and compassion to prevent the rotting of the teeth of thy humble servant Heksdokter.'

Gosling giggles, suppressing his urge to feel guilty about this blasphemy. Heksdokter's breathing becomes deep and regular.

'Through Jesus Christ our Lord, amen.'

'Did I hear you men praying?' The dominee's head pops through between the tent flap.

'No dominee,' replies Mad Dog, snapping to attention.

'Sit, sit, my boy,' says the dominee in his most paternal Afrikaans voice.

'We were all sleeping dominee.'

'I am sure I heard praying.'

'No dominee.' The dominee frowns and rubs an index finger up and down the side of his nose like an adolescent trying to buy contraceptives.

'We were all fast asleep dominee,' says Heksdokter twinkling. The dominee, looking concerned, mutters something and leaves the tent.

All four of us fall back onto our beds, bored again, still waiting for some, any, order. Mad Dog lies looking up at the ceiling. Gosling begins tinkering with his battery razor. Heksdokter continues with his *The Hound of the Baskervilles* while I start a letter to Father and Mother, being purposefully verbose in an attempt to confuse the moronic censors, using phrases like 'the quintessential question being the conundrum of our cohort's continued presence in this treacherously torpid cordon sanitaire' and 'the dilemma of who our enigmatic enemy really is.' That will fox those anglophobes, if not Father and Mother.

Heksdokter suddenly slumps off his bed and peers into the three steel helmets which hang like swollen bats from the bed frame. Each once contained several dumpy beer bottles submerged in water. He searches each helmet, finds a solitary dumpy, and opens it.

'Cheers. To the war.' He takes a long nipple-wrenching slug, collapses and again picks up his book.

'You *still* reading that book?' queries Mad Dog from his cubicle.

'Why, do you want to borrow it? Are you finally tired of your picture comics?'

Gosling giggles.

'I would like to propose that we pray that Heksdokter one day finishes that book. Any seconders?'

'Yes,' says Gosling gigglingly, sitting up in bed.

'Nimbus?'

'Abstain.' I half keep to my policy.

'Heksdokter?'

'Abstain.'

'Two for with two abstentions. The motion is carried. Three cheers for democracy.'

'Do you want to challenge?' asks Heksdokter, putting down his book and beer and holding up a humbug tin. He taps the tin; there is a frantic scrabbling inside. 'Any odds?'

'Alright.'

'Evens?'

'Okay, but with the option of double or quits.'

Heksdokter unearths a bottomless cake tin from his duffel bag and screws it into the sand in the centre of the tent. Mad Dog shakes his tobacco tin gently, infuriating its occupant. Gosling pours lighter fuel around the inner edge of the cake tin. I lie on my stomach on my bed, peering down at the preparations.

'Lay your bets,' announces Gosling, snapping his fingers.

'Four Lion dumpies.'

'Two packets of Gunston filter.'

Heksdokter opens his humbug tin and empties its contents into the arena. His scorpion is tiny and jet black. It scuttles madly about, its tail curved up over its head. He prods it with his toothbrush, feeling the impact of its sting.

'Behold Scrotum, smartest of the swiftest scorpions.' Heksdokter gulps down the remains of his beer and leans back against his rifle.

Mad Dog upends his tobacco tin. His brown scorpion flops into the arena. Its pincers and tail are huge and ponderous. It sits motionless in the middle of the tin.

'Hurray for Hubcap,' he whoops.

Gosling, as master of ceremonies, lights the lighter fuel.

129

The scorpions face each other in the ring of fire. Heksdokter's champion begins scurrying around in circles while Mad Dog's challenger dozes squatly in the centre. Gosling prods them with a bayonet. They continue their separate activities, scuttling and dozing, refusing to fight. Gosling sprinkles more lighter fuel into the arena to make the circle smaller. There is a sudden burst of flame which instantly incinerates both contestants.

'Jesus Gosling, what the fuck are you doing?' Heksdokter's and Mad Dog's shouts are simultaneous.

'Let's call it a draw,' he says quietly and slinks back to his bed.

'But you just burnt my bloody scorpion,' Heksdokter slumps onto his bed and picks up his book.

'And now what are we going to do?' asks Mad Dog with melodramatic hand gestures.

'Propose something,' I suggest, tongue-in-cheek.

Mad Dog appears briefly to sulk and then perks up fractionally. 'I think Gosling's future should be discussed. I propose . . .'

'Canteen's open!' The announcement bursts like a rifle grenade, causing immediate pandemonium. I pull on a tee-shirt and sprint after the others towards the rondavel. Behind the counter stands the Captain, punch-drunk and battered, looking more like an unsuccessful boxer than an unsuccessful boxer ever could.

'A six-pack of Lions please Captain. Is six still the limit?' It is Heksdokter's voice. The Captain frowns briefly and hands him six beers. Mad Dog sneaks into the space vacated by Heksdokter, only to be greeted by hoots and whistles from the long meandering queue which ends somewhere among the mopani trees near the gate.

'Hey, stop pushing in,' comes the chorus.

'Fuck off,' shouts Mad Dog, buying his beers.

Back in the tent I find Heksdokter, once again lying on his bed engrossed in *The Hound of the Baskervilles,* boat-racing himself through his Lions. Mad Dog lies pole-axed by his first, his arms hanging like Christmas stockings over the sides of his bed. I continue with my letter, suddenly longing more

130

than ever for home or anywhere away from the interminable waiting of this non-existence. Gosling's battery razor begins humming. Heksdokter puts down his book and scans the tent.

'Gosling, are you going to drink those two beers?'

'No.'

'Can I buy them?'

'No.' He switches his razor off and then on again.

'But they'll just get warm.'

'I don't mind warm beers.'

'I'll give you a rand a beer.'

'No, I want to save them for later.'

'Wanker.'

Gosling says nothing and continues fiddling with the innards of his razor. Heksdokter pulls on a tee-shirt and picks up his rifle. He turns to me. 'Nimbus, got a beer I can buy?'

'Sorry, this is my last. I only bought four.'

He looks across at Mad Dog but doesn't bother to ask him. He begins singing off-key that old rugby song I remember from my schooldays: 'He went to the funeral just for the ride' and leaves the tent. I notice a scorpion shuddering into the sand under my bed and crush it with my rifle butt. I continue writing, now asking the usual questions about home, knowing that the censors will probably find something subversive about something. Perhaps I too am one of the State's enemies without my knowing it. Perhaps Gosling has already reported me if he does that kind of thing. Heksdokter reappears through the tent flaps and with a 'He went down to hell where he frizzled and fried' sits down on his bed with a six-pack which he has probably bought for an exorbitant sum on the camp black-market. One of the rackets is teetotallers buying their full quota and then selling the beers at inflated prices to big-time tipplers like Heksdokter. He opens a Lion and, suddenly adopting an air of extreme gravity, begins: 'Have you chaps heard that sort of riddle about a tree falling in a forest with no one around to hear it?'

'No,' sulks Gosling, putting down the remnants of his dismembered razor.

Heksdokter downs his dumpy and tosses the empty bottle onto the floor. 'Well, if a tree falls down in a forest and there is no living thing or mammal within hearing distance, then it falls down completely silently.'

'Isn't a mammal a living thing?' asks Mad Dog.

'When did I say it wasn't?'

'You said: "and there is no living thing or mammal within hearing distance" as if living things and mammals are different.'

'Christ, you know what I mean. Things with fucken ears. That hear.' Heksdokter tugs at his earlobes. 'Like us who have to listen to your crap.'

'Anyway, about the tree,' Gosling interjects.

'Well, if there's nothing around to hear the tree fall, then it falls silently. It doesn't make a noise on its own. It just sends out sound waves which enter our ears and are then interpreted as different sounds.'

'So what?' queries Mad Dog, now amazingly animated after his recent coma.

'Your appreciation of life rests purely on your five senses. If you can't see, smell, hear, touch, or taste a girl standing near you, then, as far as you're concerned, she doesn't exist.'

'I suppose the Hound of the Baskervilles told you that one.'

'I could hardly have read it in *Captain Devil*.'

Mad Dog turns over and again submerges himself in his oblivion.

'So, basically, anything you can't sense doesn't exist for you. Like the enemy. Until we are confronted by him, he doesn't exist. It's the same principle as the girl you can't sense. She may have tits but they don't exist for you if you can't sense them. The enemy may be around. Everyone is obsessed with him. He's behind every bush but until we are confronted by him, he doesn't exist for us.'

'But every girl has some sort of tits,' whines Gosling.

'Jesus, you're one,' mumbles Mad Dog from some dark corner deep inside himself.

Heksdokter discovers that his new stock of Lions is finished and lies back on his bed. For several minutes there is silence as we muse over his philosophical jumble. Eventually he speaks: 'Fuck, everything is rigged. Either we meet our imaginary enemy and get wiped out or we lie here until we're thoroughly bush mad. Either way we lose.'

We lie in silence thinking about our predicament while a grey loerie screeches derisively at us from somewhere in the mopanis outside: 'Go-away, go-away, go-away,' until its incessant cackling becomes that of a guinea fowl — probably one of the lesser cocks condemned to a celibate existence on the periphery of the flock — which wakes me hours earlier than usual. Why that reverie of all the possibilities? Browka insists on its significance, rejecting all notions that its choice was really random. Brief mulling reveals boredom and a preoccupation with an enemy; in essence, that I feel threatened. But that is old news.

Perhaps the participants are important. All were my tent mates during that particular stint. None was fairly representative of South African stereotypes: Mad Dog, the irrational law graduate, bent on wringing every drop of black comedy from our period of militarism; Gosling, the offspring of staunchly Calvinist parents, fascist, and model conscript; and Heksdokter, the iconoclast, derisive of the system, a dipsomaniac and escaper into books. Similarly traumatised, I plodded on through the endless months, determined to make it seeing that Michael hadn't.

Of their lives after demobilisation, I know very little, as is so often the case after enforced familiarity. Mad Dog, I think, became an attorney in Johannesburg; Gosling became a civil servant in Pretoria; and Heksdokter, in an attempt to avoid doing camps, emigrated, teaching at some English public school before being killed in a charabanc accident while accompanying a cricket team on a tour of Sri Lanka.

Apart from the relevance of our analysis of both our internal and external enemies, and the coincidence that Heksdokter, perhaps like the monk, died on a road in Sri Lanka, I can glean nothing of significance. But I must take Browka's word. Consequently, I record it all as verbatim as possible, scribbling madly in bed during the remaining hours before Moses appears with the early morning tea. Its significance, I presume, will become apparent.

22

Tonight is cool. Occasional clouds scud across the glowing fires like parents shielding their children from an atrocity. Standing between the parted sliding doors with my J&B, I radar for the delicate sounds outside. The cry of the bushbaby in the flatcrown is conspicuously absent, but the others respond: quavering nightjar calls; the ubiquitous tink-tink of the fruit bats; and the distant crackle . . . the fires perhaps, or shots, or some activity at the mill. I hear the kitchen door close and Moses pad off to his room behind the stables. At precisely five-thirty tomorrow morning he will retrace his steps. Early to bed, early to rise . . . a legacy from his mission schooling, I wonder, but more likely necessity. The stove must be stoked and the milk and cream separated.

I collect a J&B bottle and siphon and move through to my study to continue this chronicle. Settling at my desk, I clear a space for my typewriter, shoving aside piles of mill reports and several unopened magazines. (Note how the illusion is revealed; everything preceding this sentence is not immediate but the past reworked.)

This evening's contribution comes slowly, needing to be drawn from within and coaxed onto the paper beneath these prodding keys. My attention is repeatedly caught by the night music and I find my fingers idle while I scan the pulsating oblong between the open shutters: darkness broken by glowing patches. Fading into a state of deep passivity with my elbows on the desk, my hands clasped in a vault above the space bar and my thumbs propped against my canines, I allow the fires to blur into rosettes, then leave them to revert. Returning to my task, I add these words and cast occasional glances at the orange patches which seem to be dulling. Stopping, I focus on them, hoping to fan their brilliance for another rosette, but their dullness increases.

I cross to the window and peer up through the flatcrown. Mottled by branches, some object is annexing the moon, a dark aggressor covering the pale aureola, inking it until only a fluorescent nail paring remains. Suddenly the penny drops. It is the eclipse mentioned in the newspaper: the lunar equivalent of the rare juxtaposition seen during the battle of Isandlwana, at the moment when the tides turned.

A torch moves up through the myrtles near my office and presently the nightwatchman, accompanied by the induna and two cutters, appears in the shadows off the veranda. We exchange greetings, then wait out the polite silence.

'Is there a problem?' I eventually probe in Zulu, knowing that there must be but playing the game.

'Yes nkosaan,' comes the soft meek chorus.

I wait in the thick silence until the induna continues. 'The moon is becoming dark and the people in the village are concerned. We came to ask of this darkness.'

I instruct them to wait, and go indoors, returning to the veranda with two tennis balls. I make the nightwatchman shine his torch horizontally and point at the beam. 'This is the light of the sun.' I hold one tennis ball in the torch light and point at its leeward side. 'This is where we are at night. These people here where the torch is shining are having daytime. They are far, beyond.' I point across the gully and out to sea.

A chorus of quiet exclamations and nodding heads follows yet I doubt whether they understand. It is more than can be expected of pupils when their teacher remains confused. I anticipate the ageless question of why, if we live on the side of a ball, is the surrounding countryside flat? It doesn't come; proof of the extent of their confusion.

'This,' I hold up the second ball, 'is the moon.' I indicate the sliver in the heavens. 'At night we can see the light of the sun shining on the side of the moon.' I hold the moon-ball beyond the line formed by the torch-sun and the earth-ball. 'Sometimes when our home gets in the way of the light of the sun, we block the light going to the moon and it becomes dark. Look,' I point up into the darkness, 'the light of the sun cannot reach it. We,' and I point at the bricked floor of

135

the veranda, 'are in the way while the sun is down there.' I stab my index finger at the floor in an attempt to add depth to my gesture. How ludicrous it seems. I turn to the men and with a tone of false conviction ask them whether they understand.

'Yes, nkosaan,' they answer simultaneously, nodding, but I am certain that they understand nothing of these celestial ramblings. The four men hesitate, reluctant to leave without their problem solved.

'There is no need to worry because the sun will be back tomorrow and when it gets dark the moon will be back again.' My conclusion seems glib after my unsatisfactory explanation.

My calmness seems to reassure them. 'Alright, nkosaan.' They say it together. They are prepared to take my word merely because I have kept all other promises. I pay them every month, I send money to their families and I open savings accounts for them. On this assumption my advice is sought and although my explanation has been worthless, they have my assurance that things will soon return to normal.

I turn but am recalled by the induna. 'Nkosaan, a man has been hurt by a pig.'

'Where?'

'Near the forest.'

Why, I ask myself, didn't he tell me this before my waffle about the eclipse. Then, I see his logic: if the world is to follow the moon into darkness, a man wounded by a pig is nothing beside this cosmic calamity.

'Who is this man?' I ask.

'Moses, nkosaan.'

I get the keys and meet them at the Land Rover. The induna climbs in beside me and the others share the back with Brutus. Turning left into the avenue of planes, I accelerate for the gully. The headlights slip across the flanking bush, revealing the matting of undergrowth. Objects on objects with their chess-like sidling into strings of roadside eclipses. What was Moses doing out here when he should have been asleep? I wonder briefly before chiding myself. Having fallen into the local malaise, I have de-humanised him, forgetting that he is an individual with his own rights. With the tend-

136

ency among the other planters to regard their employees as automatons, I have always taken a strongly contrary stance. Self interest or altruism? Slips like this make me question my motives.

A group of blacks has congregated on the contoured road across the valley from the house. Hurriedly positioning the Land Rover, I laser the dark gathering with its headlights. Remember appearances, an inner voice warns and I compose myself despite my rising panic. The group parts to let me through. Awash with blood and apparently comatose, Moses lies curled on the gravel among the cane gobbets. Beside him is his panga and several yards away slumps the carcass of the boar. The events crystallise: he had encountered the pig and in the ensuing struggle had killed it despite being gored himself. Twin gouges furrow his stomach. I kneel over him, fumbling for a pulse. The crowd cranes forward. Unable to find it at his wrist, I work my fingers into his neck. There, among the tubes and tendons, is the faint rhythm.

After years of subversive snufflings along the watercourses, the pigs have finally struck.

Placing a jersey on his wounds, we lift Moses gently onto the Land Rover and gun for the company hospital twelve kilometres away. Private planters can use it for emergencies only; all routine cases must be dealt with by the provincial hospital at Nonoti.

Passing the mill, now screened by its new security fence, we jolt through the glaring arcs and back into the darkness of the fields. The rear window is streaked with Brutus's spittle through which, in the glow of the brake lights, I can from time to time see the huddled silhouettes of the nightwatchman and cutters. Preferring sounds to silence, I natter to the induna as other planters' houses slip past and we eventually enter the bougainvillaea'd drive of the hospital.

Within minutes Moses is wheeled away by orderlies as I wait out the obligatory delay at the casualty desk. Eventually the receptionist detaches herself from the telephone, confronts me with a roneoed form, and returns to her mumbled conspiracy. I set to immediately.

Name: Moses Ndlovu

137

Reference number: —
Employer: J.D. Colville
Employer's address: Rangoon Estate, Manning's Post; and on and on, reminding me of security clearance questionnaires in the army. On completion, I abandon the form on the desk rather than risk another wait, and leave for home.

A high wind has sprung up, whining through the cane, and en route we pass one of the fires visible from the veranda earlier in the evening. As it is on company land and too far from home to demand my assistance, I detour around the jam of tractors, trailers and lorries. Pyres of smoke coil in huge wreaths from the flames, spreading themselves like further eclipses across the moon. Squads of cutters advance and retire to the commands of the indunas as several managers observe the activity from the cab roof of a hilo.

'We have had rain but there are many fires this year,' says the induna suddenly as we leave the *son et lumière* and descend past a derelict mission station. Its Catholic order, I forget which, lost favour with the government. With no new staff members able to get the necessary permits to live here, it had to close.

'Yes.'

I play my cards close to my chest, wondering if his sudden statement, preceded as it was by an interlude of silence, is rooted in inside knowledge or if it's merely a simple deduction. Seconds demand an apology; I guiltily dispel my doubt; he is undoubtedly a good person, a third generation employee on the farm, who has painstakingly worked his way up through the ranks. Fear induces an irrational response. Merely because he is black doesn't make him dishonest; I tell myself the obvious, knowing also that blood is thicker than water. Was his father or grandfather an induna? I wonder, with the sangoma's riddle still nagging me. I must check.

23

Night becomes day to become night to become day again. Time, like a chameleon, inches doggedly onwards through a banded landscape. Searing days become storms, then steamy nights. Mosquitoes hound me like furies as I go through the required motions. From behind my carefully contrived façade I watch the workings: the feverish nurturing, harvesting and milling of the cane for financial reward. The means to an end; money in the bank to give me the freedom to choose. And yet, like a mamba's mesmerised victim, I am powerless. My fate is ordained. I must press on and await some portent.

How, I now frequently ask myself, do I appear to my black employees? Am I a benign dictator who has their interests at heart or a white pig bent on their exploitation? The pendulum seems to be swinging from former to latter, oblivious of my attempts to curry favour.

It is just my luck that some enterprising forebear and his brother chose this remote corner to make a new beginning. Success came hard. The younger, Harry, met his violent end but a momentum has carried through the succeeding generations, leaving me to carry the can. Sell out, you shout, but I can't. If only things were so easy but portents cannot be had on tap.

It is a week since Moses' fateful accident; I use the adjective carefully because coincidence has its limitations. The hospital assures me that he will recover although he remains under intensive care. Peritonitis has set in but apparently the worst is past. It is now just a matter of time. More waiting. Without him, the house is a husk which I inhabit. Rose, the maid, is standing in and I make do with bangers and mash ad nauseam, but I should be thankful with so many people hungry in the district.

A man who is to me what his forebears were to mine. During the last few days solving the sangoma's riddle has

139

become more than ever my major preoccupation. Fanned by my apathy towards mundane matters, it is now an obsession. Spells of deep musing have suggested one clue to its solution and, with no other leads, I must take it. The corollary, says my little voice, is probably something well known to me but which I am blinkered from seeing. I can't see the wood for the trees, that problem.

Why, you may ask, must it be something familiar? Assuming that the sangoma is right, my deductions, as far as I can understand them, follow these lines. Here goes. The allusion to my forebears is, in all probability, limited to those who came to this country and their descendants, and not those ancestors receding deep into the history of colonial Ireland and beyond. This assumption is bolstered, I feel, by the sangoma's presumed lack of knowledge of the northern hemisphere, although I may be doing her discredit, metaphysics being disdainful of borders and oceans.

Also, bearing in mind the comparatively few whites in rural Africa, and farmers' wide contact with their black employees, it is likely that the culprit's forebear alluded to by the sangoma was a black. Here too I cannot be sure. Whites master-minded much of the subversion during the sixties, and they no doubt remain active in the recent attempts. Another ponderable becomes immediately obvious: is the present relationship and that between the forebears necessarily one between white farmers and black arsonists? There is nothing to discount two master-stablehand relationships or one of many other combinations. The relationship itself needn't include the crime which may merely have been a repeated coincidence. I can't remember either my parents or grandparents talking of an employee ever being found guilty of arson.

Based on these shaky deductions and a maze of others now blurred or forgotten, I have reached the conclusion that the arsonist is a black man whose relationship with me resembles in some way that had by one of his ancestors with either my parents or their ancestors as far back as three generations. Hardly a great lead, you may say, but it does smack of some logic, as far as that's possible in these airy-fairy matters.

140

All this I have coupled to my original assumption that the solution is probably known to me, but not seen for what it is. With this chronicle, for all its limitations, being the only mirror-image of my recent thoughts and actions, I must turn to it, reading it minutely in search of more clues.

As this riddle has puzzled me since my rendezvous with the sangoma, my subconscious must have wrestled with it continuously. If the culprit is known to me at all, then the likelihood of clues to his identity finding themselves onto these pages is high. If he is not known to me, only a chance revelation will be of any assistance.

Realising this, I decided last night to give it a try. Telling Rose that I didn't feel like supper, I sent her off early, locked myself into my bedroom, knocked back that amount of J&B which heralds lucidity and read everything, paying special attention to the pages from my visit to the sangoma onwards. My chronicle screened through my mind like a film. Halting the reel at moments that suggested tangents, I searched for collaterals before releasing it again. It took hours to complete, after which I lay back in the shuttered gloom and passed out. My subconscious, I could feel, was searching frantically. Sometime in the sleep which ensued, what I think is the answer came through to me. Like a faint morse from deep in the darkness, it pin-pointed the arsonist, corroborating the sangoma's riddle.

Consequently things look different now. My identification of the culprit has at last enabled me to assess my predicament. Many of the ponderables now fall into place. Whether my supposition is correct or not is immaterial; it is merely a catalyst for a new plan of action. Like a croquet player, I have beaten one hoop and, flushed with the achievement, can now start eyeing up its successor. And yet the comparison isn't strictly accurate; I am not bent on facing the next hoop but on avoiding it at all costs. Giving up croquet in fact; putting as much distance between myself and its hardware as possible because I know that the succession of hoops is endless. But not really giving up the game, as it were; in fact playing it with greater gusto. Don't underestimate me; I am cannier than you think.

141

Recent reflection has revealed that all my predecessors had at one time or other to make a major decision which affected their destinies: my great grandfather, after a family row, left Corsehill for Africa; my grandfather, demobilised after the Bambata Rebellion, decided to change from cattle ranching to cane cultivation; my father, after service with the KOYLIs in Burma during World War II, refused generous offers of further promotion and returned home, maintaining the continuity. Now it's my turn.

Like them at their respective times, I am now at the controls. With the yard as the hub (the many splendours of the sprawling house remain always just off centre) the farm is cycling onwards, generating ripples which radiate outwards through the multitude of stalks. Other farms do likewise, creating their own expanding circles which mesh with their counterparts, stitching this coastal strip. My ripples are thus of consequence. Our needs are mutual; hence Van Deventer's and old man Patel's concern with my actions. But I have news for them: my future actions will really be felt. My wake will buffet others. Only the decision remains to be made.

Now that much has been resolved, time is running more smoothly. Like the Land Rover emerging from the ascent out of Nonoti, it has crested, accelerating and changing up. Days slip past, appearing keen to succumb to their successors. Dawns glide to dusks. Weeks tumble. And like a towed trailer I am coupled to the pell-melling.

24

Turning and turning in the widening gyre
The falcon cannot hear the falconer;
Things fall apart; the centre cannot hold:
Mere anarchy is loosed upon the world,
The blood-dimmed tide is loosed, and everywhere
The ceremony of innocence is drowned;
The best lack all conviction, while the worst
Are full of passionate intensity.

W.B. Yeats. The Second Coming

The hospital discharged Moses this morning, nearly a month after his encounter with the pig. After parking under a sprawling flamboyant, I crossed the lawns where orderlies wheeled invalids, and entered the veranda where the less robust slumped in their regulation striped pyjamas.

'The peritonitis has gone,' the French-Mauritian doctor assured me, 'but he needs a fortnight's convalescence.' Nurses slipped past, each trim with purpose, their rubber soles squeaking on the hard plastic.

Moses sat beside me in the Land Rover. He looked older. His obvious discomfort made him appear sullen. During the journey back, he was uncharacteristically taciturn. I dropped him off at his room behind the stables.

'Krish,' I told him, 'will drive you home after you have gathered your belongings. Go carefully and I will see you next month.' As he shuffled inside I watched him briefly in the rearview mirror.

At noon I do my usual rounds, enacting to a tee my role of sugar planter. A ruddy face above faded khaki shirt and trousers. Dusty brogues with thick army-issue socks, worn like puttees as a supposed precaution against snake bites but probably useless as such. But reassuring all the same.

Orders are given and requests answered with the usual benign paternalism. As you know, I have always had my employees' interests at heart, not through any real saintliness but because indirectly they are the same as mine. Perhaps, you think, he repeats that claim too often for it to be true. Ex-ploy-ter. I can see you mouth the word but I don't give a damn. Let me put it like this: they rub my back and I rub theirs. But I call the rub, as it were.

All is apparently well with the cutters. The stalks are falling and the tractors and trailers are grinding to their system. There are no absentees and the full complement attack the steep field with vigour. Panga blades glint. The race is on. The cutters vie for the gleaming bicycle with its five speeds.

Back near the stables, Krish's assistant operates the spray-race as the stablehands prod and whistle the herd through it. Sodden and disorientated the cattle emerge from the walled pen but immediately resume their cropping. Instinct supersedes our interruptions. Nature reverts despite our tinkering. But be careful, pleads a voice, only so much can be meted out. But what do I care now?

With my mind made up, there is so much to do and yet nothing that really can be done. Surely loose ends should be tied but *why* keeps appearing and I am hard pressed to answer it. Wanting to leave the boat drifting smoothly, as it were, I must disappear with the least disturbance possible. No ripples even. Ideally, just like a crew member on the *Mary Celeste,* I must respond to the strange voice, leaving everything to the vagaries of what follows. There is a cleanliness in a quick gap. Preparations for successors only complicate things. This chronicle — my ship's log — is the only exception. Like a dead specimen preserved in formalin, it is beyond time. Consequently, like Donald Crowhurst, I am going to consciously leave it to tell the truth. Everything else will merely be left, like the footprints of a careless escapee, to speak for itself.

One thing, I told myself yesterday, must be done, but with the relief of hindsight I can now confess that it wasn't. What was to become of Brutus had begun to plague me. After hours of puzzling I made an agonising decision. Deep in the bush, not far from the scene of my recent hunting fiasco, stands an anthill. I would coax him down there, I decided, busy him with a trifle and then, with his back turned, give him both barrels. Death would be instantaneous and the ants would make short work of his mortal remains: bit by bit he would be ferried into the labyrinth until only a pale trellis remained.

All went smoothly until the *coup de grâce* when I balked. As Brutus snuffled at the seething mound, I raised the gun but couldn't pull the trigger. Magically, the overhanging foliage became monkeys and he set off in hot pursuit, his barking fading into the gully. Fateful intervention, I told myself, marvelling at its timeliness. Whatever it is that intervenes has intervened. At last things are moving. Everything augurs well for tomorrow's denouement.

Two monkeys appeared suddenly, loping into the clearing. Clambering onto the anthill, they peered into the undergrowth towards Brutus's retreat, sniffing, oblivious of my presence downwind. Slowly, smoothly, I raised the Holland & Holland and took a bead on the larger. Burst. I swung the gun fractionally . . . burst. One toppled backwards while the other vaulted into the greenness. One out of two; a fifty percent kill rate. Not good enough. Fate or whatever has again made a move, I told myself, supplying this Esau with a substitute sacrifice. The path is just visible: Brutus, forever his own, must merely continue without me.

After lunch I retire for my usual siesta. Everything so far has stuck rigidly to schedule. Even the watcher wouldn't smell a rat. With a bottle of J&B for company, I settle down in the shuttered darkness. The ice bucket is misted; beads of moisture scoot down it and onto an open book, seeping from a photograph of Lissadell — the austere Big House whose daughters went gloriously native — to Constance and Eva, the girls themselves. Slowly the sepia becomes sodden, buckling the walls and streaking the girls' kimonos. Turning onto my side, I peer obliquely from my pillow. My crystal tumbler circles the house and spilled whisky increases the warp. Had someone not immortalised them, I tell myself with the gravity of fading sobriety, all would now be lost. From Yeats I take my cue. This laboured screed is my attempt at immortality,

145

except that my gazelle is gone.

Time instils profundity, I tell myself slowly, deliberately. In years to come my account alone may preserve this facet of the ancien régime. Scholars will pore over the charred pages, fretting at the ashed edges and piecing together this ambience as it falls apart. Have I done it justice? I ask myself. Why are certain things included at the expense of others? Since reading Browka and, I think, solving the riddle from the clues in this account, certain things are clearer. I gleaned from the past only what was, and is, necessary. This meticulous selectivity, previously undetected, has with Browka's help become apparent. Everything is so much clearer now. Let me explain.

The past, being all that was, must in itself be important but random images from it dominate my memory, being somehow instilled with an added relevance. Why these apparently trivial occurrences should be elevated to almost mythic significance remains a mystery, but their very survival makes them a force to be reckoned with. Why, I often ask myself, does that incident retain its crystal clarity when even most milestones have dissolved? Perhaps the answer lies in society's imposition of a significance on apparent milestones when in reality they are nothing. Conversely, apparently meaningless incidents strike a chord and are stored — essential keys to our present selves.

With the passing of time, these incidents gradually attain their mythic status but, as nothing is static, they must face constant revision by what is actually happening. Consequently each myth faces an ongoing test and its demotion into obscurity remains a constant possibility. Much of this chronicle's significance will alter between my writing and your discovery of it. Should I still be around when you find it, much of what I have written — if, say, a decade or more has elapsed between its launching and your discovery — may surprise even me with its flatness, those mythic incidents having been succeeded by others in the interim.

My surroundings now, being the ephemeral subject which I am impelled to embalm, have memories relevant to them which must, in the nature of things, become dissipated. So, both past and present themes in this chronicle need recording.

146

Perhaps this chance of immortality will be the final straw: memories of that filtered paradise and the losing of this one will be recorded only to face possible expulsion because of the very act of their recording. Having got them out of my system, to use that hackneyed parental admonition, they must fall away. So by including them here I am both saving and losing them.

Do you see my dilemma? My joy at the completion of each chapter is tempered by a desire to jettison it. Only thoughts seem important; when they are captured, all their colour is drained. Their reflection in black and white appears vacuous. Wanting only the quintessence, I am tempted to destroy each folio. And yet, like the exquisitely executed apsaras at sphinx-like Sigiriya, each is timeless. I must, I tell myself, think beyond to when this mundaneness has become exotic. It is my duty, says a voice, while an echo demands ruthlessness. I falter briefly, then, in a flash of clarity, decide: despite their shortcomings, I will retain these pages, roll them up and fit them snugly into the cylinder. That is the limit of my responsibility. Whether they are found or not is Fate's decision. I have done my bit. Like Pilate, I now wash my hands of the matter.

Now, with two hours to tea time, I must sleep. Farmwork runs down in the early afternoon heat but the knowledge that I will be doing my rounds at dusk helps maintain a momentum. So meticulous has been my charade that there can't be an inkling that I won't be on schedule. Perhaps this evening, of all evenings, has my name on it. The trap will be laid but never sprung. Faceless figures will melt into the bush to return another day. But I have news for them: there won't be another; their wait will be a long one. I won't be butchered at the crossroads. I am a bad bet anyway. Killing me is no achievement. Sitting, as I am, squarely on the fence, only death will enforce an allegiance; the side on which I fall will depend entirely on the blow. Should the system get me, I will die a freedom fighter; should the freedom fighters be responsible, I will merely be another fascist getting his just deserts. But neither will.

After sleep I wake. My only proof of the former is my

147

watch's advance. What said two o'clock now says nearly four. Time that is unaccounted for must, I assume, be sleep. Rose taps on the door. 'Master, tea is served.' Pure Ceylon and rock-cakes, the usual fare. Despite the flux, some things hold out.

Why not go out with a bang? I ask you and myself. Cock a final snook. Rose isn't a bad looker. I see myself slipping down her panties — Andrea's cast-offs more than likely — and having my way on the scullery floor. Rutting my dark Rosaleen. Providing she consents of course. Raping a black is too condonable. A mutually consented to master-servant relationship is another ball game. Like Harry's possible liaison with the Hamilton's ayah, its implications are threatening. Blacks and whites can lust for each other and consummation is possible. The rigid limits can be transgressed. Our cover of exclusiveness can be blown.

After my departure there is bound to be some kind of investigation. The police will comb the house and interrogate the employees. Rose will be a major suspect. Her attempts at an alibi will be weighed and analysed. S'major van Deventer will encourage loquaciousness, goading her on with barbs and pleasantries. Perhaps, with her rising gall, she will blurt it out, telling all of our tumble beneath the helter-skelter of mousse moulds. Cheeky kaffir. Seducing her baas and then killing him. Where did you dump his body? In the cane fields, I suppose.

Alas, you know as well as I do that Rose will remain inviolate. Such thoughts will remain merely such. Titillating musings are my limit. Some do without thinking while others think without doing. Being one of the latter, my forthcoming action will seem strangely incongruous. But it won't really be. Like a gnarl of flotsam the flood has borne me on and I go where I must.

Word will filter through to the district who, radiantly sanctimonious, will at last have their suspicions confirmed. He had it coming to him; a child that plays with fire is bound to burn its fingers. But let them think what they like.

At precisely five to six, I, James Colville, your protagonist, fresh from a shower and dressed in beige trousers, a white

148

shirt and a maroon cravat, appear on the veranda. Omitting yet again to switch on the radio, I turn to the drinks tray which Rose has arranged so meticulously. Like Moses, she has learnt my idiosyncracies and caters for them. The J&B bottle, flanked by the soda siphon and ice bucket, looms over the dishes of peanuts and biltong slivers. How well my hand and the curved green bottle perform, like intimates of long standing. In a flash the first of my last sundowners is prepared. Forgive the apparent melodrama, it isn't intended; I am being as lucid as possible, not for myself but for the record. Being so near to the end of this chronicle, I cannot afford to falter.

As if on cue, the night begins to assert itself, gradually edging out distractions until it is everything. Like sand in an hour-glass, one bulb gaining at the expense of the other, acuteness welling up. Zigzagging bats radar and I reciprocate, deflecting their sonar, entwining it with the other night music: cricket-shrillings, bushbuck-barkings; nightjar-quaverings; owl-hootings, monkey-chatterings and the muffled throbbing of the tom-toms in the valley.

Down the lawn, beyond the bank of azaleas, the steep orchard and the contour road, is the cane. Swivelling my wicker chair, I glimpse the arrows through a gap in the mango trees. Their softness is hard in the settling darkness, chromed with moonlight. They are swaying slightly on their stalk-shafts, each rasping its neighbour and adding its tiny whisper to the hush. Friend or foe? I wonder fleetingly. Assegais or bayonets? Every night the camouflaged battalions occupy the foothills, new arrows swelling their ranks, awaiting orders. With the mills barely operating, we are powerless to attack in defence. Instead we retreat indoors and leave them to it.

At seven o'clock the gong calls and I follow. Rose appears, spruce in her pink uniform and white apron, offering a split avocado which I sprinkle with cinnamon and sugar, scooping the green flesh and washing it down with riesling. Then rump steak with mash and marrows. I have at last been weaned off bangers but the mash persists. Then cheese and biscuits, then coffee. She is wonderfully attentive, materialising from the scullery at the moment the bell tinkles. Her hands, honey-

149

brown, place plates on the mats with the deftness of a draughts player in a needle game. She is, I notice, particularly attentive to my requests. Perhaps she likes me. Perhaps I'm not a jerk employer. If there was more time, perhaps my musings could have materialised. Without Andrea they would need to be.

I return to the veranda for a couple more shots before retiring to my study to record today for posterity. Put it on the map, as it were. Reveal it to those codgers who will mull over it and declare with profundity that life was leisured before the transition.

The cane is nearer now, just below the azaleas. Its expectant hush, like that of an impi before battle, buffets me as I pour my penultimate tot. Brutus snuffles out of the darkness, collapsing at my feet and begins to lick himself noisily. In the distance near KwaZulu several fires slit the darkness, their lengthening glows conjuring the advancing arrows into jagged silhouettes. I pour my last tot, a double. The cane is nearer still. Like a guileful predator stalking its prey, it advances whenever I am not looking, then freezes under my stare. With the hum cool and distant I have no ally. I must merely watch as my immobile attacker nears. Or conduct a tactical retreat, a retrograde action, which I do, moving through to my study as previously scripted.

Warping time yet again, I record this chapter with its present-tense immediacy from midway, pretending the past is now present which it never really is. Future too must remain such; my jottings about it comprise the script for my succeeding actions. Only the act of writing is honestly present, its subject matter being a kite launched by me but now drifting slowly ahead and dragging me on. With my pattering typewriter tracing its methodical progress (like George Yeats's, my writing is now automatic), I cast a last look at the book-lined walls with their familiar mosaic of coloured spines, the team photographs, the Isandlwana portrait and the scattering of ramrods, two-by-fours and the bottles of gun oil, all of which, I suppose, will tell a story. Detectives will scan the volumes for clues, noting the few examples of banned literature — erotica and politics — seeing them not as a miniscule proportion of all, but as irreproachable proof that I was subversive. Bully for them; the last laugh will still be mine.

The kite is pulling away, the typewriter tapping its account of how I carefully place this last chapter under all the preceding pages, slip it into an envelope, seal it, and put it in turn into the asbestos cylinder. Lifting the Persian prayer-mat beneath the battle scene, I open the trapdoor, snap on the light, and descend into the cellar. Rows of wine bottles point accusingly as I edge several rieslings aside, exposing the mossy fissure, and ease the cylinder deep into it. Moss fragments, scuffed by the slow insertion, patter onto the lower rows. Scooping them into my handkerchief, I flick them back inside, reluctant to leave too many clues. Replacing the bottles across the entrance, I scrutinise the array, making certain that everything is as it was, before switching off the light. Contrasting waves of elation and sadness buffet me as I climb the stairs. Doubts well up. Am I doing the right thing? The question demands an answer. Without conviction I answer in the affirmative, knowing that the chronicle demands it for my sake. The wheel has turned and is about to turn again.

The arrowing cane has reached the veranda, its vanguard hushing along the flagstones. Both the mill lights and those of the company houses have disappeared, leaving only the filtered glows of the fires. Suffused with the orange light the plumes nod menacingly through the shutters like villains in a shadow play.

My time has played out; only the depositing of the cylinder hasn't yet run the gauntlet of the ratchets. The wheel keeps on turning, the film snickers on, tugging me into the eyepiece. I must be going now.

Glossary

amatungulu: evergreen shrub with waxy leaves and red fruit (from Zulu *amathungulu*)

apsara: heavenly maiden

bandarlog: monkeys (Monkey-People from Kipling's *Jungle Book*)

bateleur: eagle with characteristic flight

boomslang: venomous, arboreal snake (Afrikaans)

dassie: rock hyrax (Afrikaans)

dominee: minister of the Dutch Reformed Church (Afrikaans)

flufftail: smallish bird frequenting marshes and forest edges

guti: wet, misty weather (from Shona *makute*)

hilo: large lorry used for transporting cut sugar cane

imfino: wild spinach (Zulu)

induna: headman, supervisor (Zulu)

kaffirboetie: nigger lover, negrophile (from Afrikaans *kafferboetie*)

KwaZulu: Zululand (literally 'Place of the Zulu') (Zulu)

kwela: penny-whistle music (from Nguni *khwela*)

leguaan: iguana, monitor lizard

mopani: common tree or shrub in low rainfall areas

muti: African medicines, also used in witchcraft (from Zulu *uMuthi*)

153

nkosaan: master, sir (from Zulu *nkosana*)

nkosazaan: madam, lady (from Zulu *nkosazana*)

pooja house: Hindu shrine

rotavator: machine with rotating blades designed to break up soil

sangoma: soothsayer, diviner (Zulu)

sittara: Sinhalese artist, painter

spanspek: sweet melon, cantaloupe (Afrikaans)

spreeu: starling (Afrikaans)

stompie: cigarette butt (Afrikaans)

tambotie: indigenous tree, the wood of which is extensively used for furniture

togt: casual or day labour (Afrikaans)

umdoni: indigenous tree usually found near water (Zulu)

umfaan: boy (Zulu)

umlungu: white man (Zulu; plural: *abelungu*)

ABOUT THE AUTHOR

John Conyngham is a sub-editor on the *Natal Witness* newspaper in South Africa. *The Arrowing of the Cane* is both his first novel and the first part of a trilogy; it was awarded the prestigious 1988 Olive Schreiner Prize. In his early thirties, John Conyngham is married with two children.